Content Note

This novel includes depictions of sexual violence and its aftermath.

While the assault itself is not described in graphic detail, the story contains on-page memories/flashbacks, sensory triggers (e.g., door sounds, restraint, dissociation), and sustained exploration of trauma, recovery, and PTSD. Additional potentially distressing content includes stalking/harassment (letters and proximity), medical trauma involving a child (cancer treatment, transplant), panic attacks, a structure fire, physical violence/underground fighting, substance misuse, and the death of a parent on the page.

If you prefer to avoid intense scenes, know that the assault is referenced throughout and is most concentrated in the middle and late sections of the book; skimming these moments will not prevent you from following the plot.

Please take care of yourself while reading. If you or someone you know needs support, consider reaching out to local services. Resources include:

- Beyond Blue (1300 22 4636 | beyondblue.org.au)

- AU: 1800RESPECT (1800 737 732 | 1800respect.org.au)

- Lifeline (13 11 14 | lifeline.org.au)

- National Alcohol and Other Drug Hotline (1800 250 015 | health.gov.au)

- StandBy Support After Suicide (1300 727 247 | standbysupport.com.au)

Your wellbeing matters more than any book.

For my grandfather — the old man whose

favourite line was always, "Who cares."

It took me years to understand what you meant.

Because every time you said it while I was crying,

you were already making me coffee,

spoiling me with ice cream and hot food,

putting on movies that made me laugh,

and insisting the cheesecake and iced coffees

"just fell into the trolley."

Thank you for showing me that love lives in

actions

far more than in words.

For supporting me when no one else would.

For believing me when others didn't.

For being my lighthouse

in every storm I didn't think I'd make it

through.

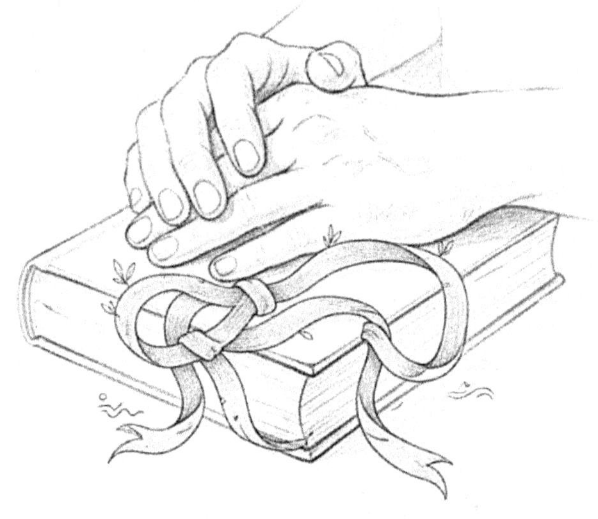

For the ones who learned that healing isn't a
straight line but a green ribbon – frayed, tied, retied
pulling you toward tomorrow.

For the broken, the bruised, the brave —

not because you fought, but because you stayed.

May your healing come in pieces, as small as breath

and as stubborn as hope.

To the reader who picked this up, while holding more than a book.

I see the weight in your hands., I see the ache you don't name.

This story is yours now too — take what you need,

leave the rest.

For the ones who weren't believed.

For the ones who weren't protected.

For the ones who kept breathing anyway.

For every survivor who learned to fight, when all you wanted was

rest.

For the rage you swallowed, for the softness you saved,

for the future you still deserve.

For the ones who learned that healing isn't a straight line

but a green ribbon — frayed, held, tied, retied —

pulling you toward tomorrow.

You are seen. You got this

Chapter One:

Always Running

The sun glints off the steel gate in my rear-view mirror until it's nothing but a blur. I keep staring until the farm shrinks to fence posts and rust, each post flashing like frames of a film I don't belong in anymore. My foot sinks harder on the accelerator. If I stop now, I'm not sure I'll start again.

The money from Mum and Dad's deaths is supposed to be enough for a new start. A house deposit someday. A safety net. For now, it's survival: rent, uniforms, groceries. Enough to keep Charlie fed until I figure out how to be everything she's lost. The math works on paper but never in my chest.

Charlie thinks I'm running—from grief, from the weight of everything unsaid. Maybe she's right. But I'm also running from the town itself. Gossip there never dies; it breeds.

With our parents gone, staying would mean questions I can't answer, whispers I can't stop.

The first spit of city rain freckles the windscreen. Copper floods my tongue for half a heartbeat — my brain's favourite trick.

Beside me, Charlie sleeps with her hood low, one hand curled against the window. Even in dreams her jaw is stubborn. She's fifteen, almost sixteen, brilliant and reckless. She could build worlds if the world didn't keep breaking her first.

She's fragile and fierce. And she's mine to protect now.

I grip the wheel tighter. I'm twenty-three. Too young to be anyone's guardian. Too old to still feel like a child myself. Now I'm big sister, stand-in mum, reluctant father figure all rolled into one. I don't know how to do it. Some days I can barely breathe. But quitting isn't an option. The old seatbelt scar above my collarbone burns beneath my shirt like a reminder of the rules that kept me alive.

By the time the skyline rises, my back aches. The building is easy to find—cheap rent, two bedrooms, close to trams and closer to the bar where I have an interview tomorrow. Inside smells of paint and cleaning spray, faint lemon undercut with dust. The scent jabs memory—Mum's hands after the dishes—but passes quick.

Boxes line the walls. The rooms echo when we talk. Unpacking feels like pulling teeth. Every item is a reminder—family photos, Mum's crocheted blanket, Dad's dented thermos. They don't warm the space;

they just underline absence. I force frames onto shelves anyway. Small vows, even if I don't believe them.

Charlie drifts through the apartment like a ghost. She avoids her room, lingers on the window seat near the kitchen bench, sketching. I don't press. She'll claim it when she's ready.

That first night, silence presses heavy. Every creak feels like warning. I lie awake counting the gaps between Charlie's breaths. A siren ghosts the street below. Copper touches the back of my throat and fades.

Sleep takes me in jolts, dropping me back into the night that made the notch above my collarbone.

Then

Rain lashed the city until every streetlight wore a crown of sparks. I told myself I'd head home after one more song, then after one more bad decision. By eleven-o-seven I was a promise-breaker under the servo awning, phone gasping for charge, watching taxis spit water and boys spit promises.

Nine missed calls. Two messages from Charlie, both the same word: Cas?

I called home. Mum answered like she'd been holding the phone already.

"Cas?"

"I'm sorry," I blurted. "Can you… come get me?"

She didn't ask the questions she could've. Just: "Where are you?"

"The servo by the overpass." I tried a joke about the flicker in the DIESEL sign. She let it slide.

"You wait there. Don't talk to anyone. Ten minutes."

Headlights turned the corner. My bones recognised the bonnet before my eyes did. Dad at the wheel, Mum leaning forward like urgency could shorten distance. Relief cracked me open.

I slid in. Lemon detergent and Dad's mint gum wrapped around me. "You, okay?" Charlie asked, small, not accusing.

"I'm okay," I lied. Her sneaker tapped my boot. I'm here. I'm here.

"Seatbelt," Mum said, because some sentences hold the world together.

Yellow light from a string of lamps brushed across us. For a moment, we looked whole. "Chips tomorrow," Charlie mumbled.

"Chips tomorrow," Mum said.

"Chips tomorrow," I echoed, tucking the promise into my chest.

Then headlights flared, too close, too fast. The night narrowed to a single bright line—

Now

The kettle clicks. Morning drags me toward Take Flight. Tomorrow's worries— rent, bills, criminology degree slipping further away—gnaw at me. Dreams have expiration dates, and mine just smudged further away.

But today there's only one job: survive, and keep Charlie breathing.

Chapter Two:

Take Flight

The city is louder at night, every sound sharpened. Neon leaks across wet pavement, taxis spit curses, music hums from open doors. By the time I step into Take Flight, nerves hum under my skin like static.

Inside is a storm of glass clinks, laughter, citrus and beer. Emily waves me over, grin quick, hair tied back. "Slice duty," she orders, sliding a crate of lemons across the bar.

I fall into rhythm: slice, twist, drop. Citrus clings sharp to my fingertips. For the first time since moving, I almost feel useful.

From the side room, a piano wakes. Notes slip out—hesitant, then sure. The crowd hushes. I glance over.

Chase sits at the keys, jacket off, sleeves rolled. Scars ladder his forearms like pale lightning. He doesn't look at anyone, but the room leans toward him. His music steadies my ribs before I can stop it.

The door opens. A broad-shouldered man enters, scar down his jaw. Emily waves him over. "Cas, this is Jesse. Security. Looks scary, but he's a teddy bear."

He grips my hand firm. "Lasted a week already? Tougher than you look."

"I lasted twenty-three years," I reply. His brow lifts; Emily snorts.

Hours pass in blur—orders shouted, glasses sliding, sweat and laughter thick in the air. For a while I'm not the orphan guardian. I'm just Cas, bartender.

Emily leans close, whispering, "He's watching you." Her eyes flick to the piano.

I glance over. Chase's eyes aren't on the keys. They're on me. Scars visible, but so is the steadiness. When he catches me staring, he nods once. Something tightens and loosens at once in my chest.

Break comes late. I step into the alley, grateful for damp air. My phone buzzes:

Still alive. Found a bookstore. Might never come home.

Relief. I type: *Don't make me file a missing persons report on day one.*

The door creaks. Jesse steps out, lighter sparking. "You don't smoke?"

"Running's my poison."

"Better one." His gaze is sharp, not cruel. "You look like someone waiting for the next hit."

My chest tenses. "What makes you think there's a next?"

"Because you're out here instead of eating inside. People don't run unless something's chasing them."

His words trip the padlock in my head. Rain needles the windshield. Headlights explode white. The seatbelt bites down. Dad's last nod—

Now

A bin slams inside; the piano coughs awake. I pocket the shaking and return to the noise.

Hours later, when chairs stack and bottles clink, Emily corrals us into a booth. Pizza boxes, grease-stained napkins, cheap soda. For the first time in months, I laugh.

Chase joins last, shadows under his eyes. He watches before he speaks. "You did good tonight," he says.

I nod, voice stuck.

Emily throws a crust at him; he lets it hit. The table erupts in laughter.

Grief loosens its chokehold, just for a beat.

Back at the apartment, Charlie sprawls on the couch, bookstore bag at her feet. She shrugs when I tuck a blanket around her. "City's better than I thought. Nobody stares at my eyes here."

I smile into the dark. For once, the city doesn't feel like it's swallowing us. It feels like maybe it could carry us forward.

Charlie's POV – Corridor Math

Then

Hospitals always smell like lemons pretending to be something else. This one was extra-lemon because the night nurse had mopped just before dawn, turning the corridor into a wet, shining river I wasn't allowed to step in. I sat on a hard chair that made my hips ache and held Cas's jacket to my face until it learned my breathing.

They wrapped Cas's hands like she was a present no one knew how to open. Tweezers found glass; the brown sting made a smell like pennies melting. Cas watched the ceiling like there were instructions in invisible ink.

Mum was behind a curtain. When they wheeled her past, she was grey at the edges like someone had started erasing and got tired.

The nurse told me I could walk with her, so I did, even though I felt unhooked from gravity. I counted ceiling tiles because numbers are little boats.

A woman called Trish arrived—cardigan, lanyard, gentle eyes. "I'm the social worker." She sat where my chair ended, hands folded like teachers waiting for a class to be brave.

"I need to talk to you about paperwork," she said, and then looked at me. "Both of you, if that's okay."

We went to a small room with a window staring at brick. She turned a form for Cas and gave her a pen with teeth marks in the cap. "You're twenty-three," she said, not asking. "You can sign for your mother."

Cas looked at her bandaged hands. "I can't hold it," she murmured, embarrassed, like telling a stranger you can't swim.

Trish nodded, looked at me. "You're fifteen?"

I nodded. My throat felt like the hallway—polished but dangerous.

"As Charlie's next of kin, you'll be recorded as her guardian," Trish said. She said guardian like it was a hat anyone could wear. The word flew around the room, landed in my lap, refused to move.

"Oh," I said. Then, "Okay."

We found a way to sign—my hand holding the pen, her bandages guiding my wrist. Her letters were small and careful, learning how to be a name. She said "sorry" three times; I said "don't" four.

Back in the corridor, lemon had been joined by coffee and plastic raincoats. People arrived wet, with eyes that couldn't settle. Everyone spoke in the voice that doesn't wake babies.

They let us see Mum. Her arm was a bright map of tape. She opened her eyes like the lids were heavy. I held the bed rail so I wouldn't float off and stick to the ceiling like a balloon. Cas leaned in and pressed her forehead to Mum's; they breathed together, like swimming lessons.

A man in black with a kind mouth said he was very sorry and then said Dad's name and the room tilted. I had thought if I didn't say the word out loud it couldn't find the door. He said it and it walked in and sat on my chest.

Mum made a noise I'd only heard once—when she saw bone. Cas made no noise. She leaned on her wrapped hands like praying. Her shoulders shook; nothing came out.

Trish brought two hot chocolates with skins. She blew mine and said drink this. I did because it was a sentence I could carry. I held the cup for Cas and she made a baby joke that fell apart at the end. We laughed anyway. Laughing is glue.

By morning the corridor decided to be a corridor again instead of a tunnel. Cas signed three more things. I signed one. Guardian sat between us like a stubborn pet we were learning to feed.

We passed a vending machine. Cas stared at the swirled bars like she'd forgotten what they were. "Chips tomorrow," she said to the part of last night where everything was still yellow and soft.

"Chips tomorrow," I said, because you can keep promises across days if you hold them tight enough.

The floor had dried but the mop's path still showed, shiny in places, a map of a country we didn't want to visit. We followed it anyway, because what else do you do.

What I noticed but didn't say:
On the far side of the ward a woman in a dark coat leaned against the pay-phone, head bowed, whispering fast. I'd seen her once at Dad's hardware store talking to Eli. Her eyes flicked up when she heard his name on the doctor's lips, then slid away. The way adults slide when something isn't for kids.

I filed it like I file numbers—tile counts, heartbeats, names of kids at school who hiss *Freak Eyes* when they think I can't hear. They don't know numbers are boats. They don't know boats can cross rivers.

I held Cas's jacket tighter. The fabric smelled like rain, like lemon trying to be something else, like change.

Chapter Three:

The Quiet Between

Doors

Morning breaks thin and grey, the sky the colour of unwashed glass. The cheap stovetop pot sputters like it might give up, coughing steam across the benchtop. Toast burns at the edges. The apartment still smells of paint and cleaning spray—lemon under dust—like a rental that hasn't learned our shapes yet. The scent reaches for an old place in me—Mum's hands—and then lets go.

Charlie appears in her hoodie, sleeves swallowing her hands. She pretends she isn't nervous, but her mismatched eyes—blue and brown—give her away. They find the light and dare it to blink first.

"It's orientation," I say, sliding the better slice onto her plate. "Not the Hunger Games."

She tears a napkin into confetti. "You don't know that."

"I know high schools. Fluoro lights. Teachers who insist on 'Charlotte' even after you correct them. Someone promises a shortcut and gets everyone lost." I nudge a banana closer. "Text me when you get there."

"Obviously." Which, in Charlie, means if I remember.

I butter the toast I'm not hungry for. "You look good," I add. "Cool. Mysterious. Dangerously literate."

She fights a smile and loses. "You look like you slept in your clothes."

"Accuracy is your superpower." I sip coffee and try to look like I've slept. "I'm on close tonight."

She rolls the napkin into a rope. "Don't wait up. I might go back to that bookstore."

There's an edge there—freedom pressed against the glass of safety. Pick the wrong words and it shatters.

"Text your route. And if plans change."

She sighs sharp but not cruel. "Okay."

We eat in companionable silence. The building's plumbing moans somewhere in the walls. Down the hall, someone argues with a kettle. Normal sounds. The best kind.

At the door she hesitates, fussing with her laces. I tuck a strand of hair behind her ear. "You've got this," I say.

Her eyes check my face for a lie. Finding none, she nods, chin high, and goes.

The apartment exhales. I fold the baby blanket Mum crocheted and pretend my eyes don't sting. Then I braid my hair tight, pull on black clothes that don't show spills, and catch the tram.

Outside, the city scrolls by: an old woman in a canary scarf whacking a vending machine like it owes her money; a tradie watering defiant grass; two girls rehearsing a TikTok under a shop awning, laughter ricocheting off glass. Everyone surviving their own way.

Take Flight looks different by day. Without the buffer of music and bodies, its history shows—dents in the counter, scratches in the boards, a jukebox that wheezes two notes before dying. Sun catches dust like confetti in freefall.

Emily claps once. "Crash course. You're on close."

She moves like a drill sergeant fuelled by lollies. We run the list: cash up, keg pressure, glasswasher vinegar rinse, spouts soaking, float counted, bathrooms checked, the unloved job of de-sticky-ing the patch of floor behind the left tap where cider went to sugar heaven.

"And the back door," she says, voice flattening. "Never prop it open. Ever. If it sticks, you don't muscle it. You call me, Chase, or Jesse. Promise."

"I promise."

We walk the service corridor. Fluoro buzzes with a permanent headache. The back door sulks—steel, security bar, paint scuffed to metal near the latch. Emily lifts the bar, swings it hard, listens. The latch catches with a stubborn clunk.

"See? Fussy." She jiggles it, smacks the push plate like it offended her. "We've told Chase to book a locksmith."

"He said tomorrow," Jesse adds, appearing from nowhere, hands in pockets, calm wound tight. He puts his weight into the door the way you quiet a horse—nothing sudden, all certainty—then checks the frame. "Until then, you swing twice. You hear the latch. You check the latch."

"The last lock," Emily says. The phrase sits between us heavier than it should.

I nod. My hands are steady. My heart isn't.

As we turn back, Emily scoops up her tote. It yawns open; a small white bottle bumps the seam—folate tablets, label half-scuffed. She zips the bag without comment, thumb lingering on the pull like it's a secret she's keeping from herself too.

We loop through Cupid's Wing. In daylight the piano looks like a secret left in plain sight. Lid up; wood nicked and loved and a little out of tune. I run a finger along the keys without pressing. It feels like a boundary. A promise.

Emily thumps the jukebox; it coughs a chord like a ghost clearing its throat.

"Haunted," she declares.

"Ghosts are easier than people," Jesse says, deadpan.

I don't laugh.

By late afternoon the bar breathes again. A table of nurses order espresso martinis with the reverence of the nearly-undead. Three tradies claim the corner like a campsite. A couple in early-date territory negotiate olives like a treaty.

My apron buzzes.

Made it.

Teacher has a curtain fringe.

People stared. It's fine.

Found the art room. Smells like glue heaven.

Buy milk?

I send a thumbs-up, doubt it immediately, add a heart, then hate myself for being that parent and drop the phone like it might explode.

Chase drifts toward Cupid's Wing at dusk, sleeves rolled, scars pale against his skin. He sits and coaxes sound out like he's apologising to the instrument for waking it. The bar hushes a millimetre. He plays for himself more than for us. I like that. It feels honest. The notes line up with my breath before I ask.

He glances up, catches me watching. Doesn't pretend he didn't. Lifts his chin, a small nod, and returns to the keys. It lands somewhere I don't have a word for.

I overpour a gin; Emily's knuckles find my elbow. "Oi. Face in the game."

"Yes, Manager."

She beams at the title like it's a joke and a crown.

The room thins from voices to coats to the imprint of bodies on vinyl. Chairs flip onto tables like skeletons doing headstands. The music dies; the air relaxes. My feet ache in the good way.

We divide and conquer. I stack glassware, count the float, duck for a fallen coaster and crack my head on the bar hard enough for stars. Emily swears on my behalf and hands me a tea towel full of ice. Jesse vanishes to his ritual bathroom sweep. From Cupid's Wing, the piano lid lowers with a soft thud; I picture Chase's hands hovering before he lets night go.

Emily's phone blooms light: Reminder — GP follow-up. Two little hearts where exclamation marks might be. She swipes it away like shooing a moth. "Tomorrow's already loud," she tells no one.

I haul a crate of empties down the corridor. Fluoro hum, mop slosh, the building's bones muttering. At the back door I set the crate down, press the bar, and pull.

Locked. Good.

I breathe. Swing once. Hear the latch. Swing again. Hear it catch. Palm-check the cold metal where the paint has rubbed thin. Solid.

On the way back a bottle nicks the crate lip and pops free, cracking against the concrete. I flinch—too big for a small thing.

"All good?" Jesse calls, already moving.

"Fine," I say, heat in my cheeks. "Making sure the ghosts feel included."

He huffs a laugh but scans the dark anyway. "We're nearly done."

"Then bed," I say.

"Then bed," he echoes, like a treaty.

The corridor goes quiet in the wrong way. Not the sticky reverb of a badly hung door, not wind messing around. A single, exact shake shivers the back door. Metal on metal, patient. Like a key that doesn't belong trying its luck.

"Cas?" Emily's voice floats from the bar, breezy until it's not. "You good?"

My mouth forgets how to say yes. "Someone's at the door," comes out as a breath.

Jesse is thunder, then nothing—the way big men move when they've learned to. He leans his ear to the steel. One Mississippi. Two. He looks at me and nods: there's a plan and I'm in it.

He unseats the bar and throws the door wide.

Cold night spills in. Bins crouch under the eaves, a cat bolts, a bottle rolls lazy across concrete and taps the brick. The air smells of damp cardboard and rain-wet bitumen.

No one.

Emily arrives with the torch from under the bar, beam slicing the alley. She hands it to Jesse, then tows my crate out of the walkway with a gentle scowl like I've personally offended OH&S.

"What happened?" she asks without sugar.

"The door rattled," Jesse says. "She heard it. Scrape too."

Emily's eyes cut to mine. Not dismissing. Assessing. "You okay?"

"I'm fine," I say. It's more wish than lie.

Chase comes last, tie off, sleeves rolled, hair mussed from his own hand. His gaze goes from me to the door and back. The night sits in his eyes like he swallowed it. There's the faintest limp in his step he hides by turning it into swagger. When the torch hits the alley, a muscle in his jaw ticks; he looks away like his bones remember other corridors with other doors.

"Locked?" he asks, already checking.

"Was," Jesse says. "Still is."

Chase tests it anyway. It's the same particular tension, as if this door owes him something and refuses to pay. He jiggles the handle, swings, listens. The latch catches. His hand stays a beat longer than the demo needs, as if bargaining with steel.

"Locksmith," he says. "Tomorrow."

"Been saying tomorrow for weeks," Emily mutters.

He ignores her. His gaze settles on me, steady. No platitudes. Just rope.

"If it sticks again," quiet so it's only for me, "you call me. Doesn't matter the hour. You don't check it alone. Got it?"

My throat works. "Got it."

He nods once. "Good."

We finish shut-down faster than my pulse will listen. I triple-check the till, then check nothing because my hands are shaking and counting has turned into rocket science. The apartment door will get locked twice tonight, then a third time after I'm in bed and convinced I dreamed the first two.

On the tram, my reflection rides the window—jaw tight, hair frizzed from steam, eyes too wide. I look older than twenty-three.

Older than someone who says I've got this and is believed.

At home, Charlie sprawls on the couch with a school map crumpled under her shoulder and the bookstore bag half-open. I tuck a blanket around her and pull the map free. In the bottom corner, someone's drawn a tiny dragon in biro. It grins with fangs.

Steam fogs the bathroom mirror. Hot water needles my shoulders. When I close my eyes, I still hear it: metal on metal. My fists press to tile until the heat stops helping.

In the mirror, I tell the girl who looks like me, "Get stronger."

She doesn't argue. But she doesn't look convinced.

Chapter Four:

Fault Lines

By Friday, Take Flight feels like second skin. My hands reach for bottles without thought; my feet adjust to the give of the mats; the burn in my calves borders on satisfying. Routine is medicine. Keep moving. Keep pouring. Don't stop long enough to think.

"Three days in and you're faster than half the staff," Emily whistles as I line up four drinks in one sweep.

"That's… comforting," I mutter, sliding the tray.

"Not a lie though." She grins. "Some coast. You don't. You run."

She isn't wrong. Running is the only thing I've ever been good at.

The jukebox cuts mid-song as the door swings and a gust of perfume slaps me—

sharp, expensive, engineered. A woman strides in like she owns oxygen. Heels click like metronomes for gunfire, sequins at her throat scatter light. She doesn't look at the bar. Doesn't need to. Her eyes are already fixed on Chase, who's near the jukebox with Jesse. She threads herself onto his arm with the entitlement of someone who's practised.

"That's Amelia," Emily says, voice flat as a blade.

Amelia leans in, whispers something that tightens Chase's jaw. His smile doesn't reach his eyes. When his gaze lifts, it finds me—only a heartbeat—before sliding away.

Amelia notices. Of course she does. Her stare drifts across the room, deliberate, like she's choosing which piece of me to carve first. Then she smiles. It isn't kind.

Later, when the bar is a tide, Amelia drops an empty like a summons. "White wine. Cold."

I pour, neutral.

"So, you're the stray," she says, scrolling her phone.

My hand falters. "Excuse me?"

"Emily brings them in sometimes. Chase is too soft to say no." She lifts the glass, sips slow, lets silence stretch. "Don't get comfortable. He gets bored."

The words sting harder than spirits. Before I reply, Jesse appears like a wall. "Don't you have somewhere better to be, Amelia?"

Her smile drips sugar. "Nowhere better than here." She trails crimson nails along the bar as if to leave scratches, then drifts back to Chase.

Jesse watches her go. "Ignore it. She eats reactions."

Easy to say. My pulse is still tap-dancing.

Saturday, Charlie comes home like weather. Backpack hits the floor; frames rattle. She vanishes to her room. Bass thumps through the door a minute later.

I hover outside, knuckles ready, then let my hand drop. She'll talk when she's ready.

Dinner is pasta she doesn't want. She shoves it around. Finally: "Some girls asked if I wear contacts to make my eyes look freaky. Said I'm trying too hard to be special."

The words slice. "And you said?"

"That it's genetic." Shrug. Stab. "They laughed anyway."

Heat spikes under my ribs. "Idiots. Your eyes are beautiful. Unique is strong."

She doesn't look up. "Doesn't feel like it."

I want to hug her, to build a wall with my body. Instead, I grip the fork till the metal complains. "One day it will. Until then— you've got me."

Her eyes flash. "You don't get it."

I swallow the lump. "Maybe not. But I'm trying."

Glue-thick silence. Then she pushes the bowl away. "Can we get ice cream?"

Relief flickers. "Yeah. Yeah, we can."

On the street, the night drizzles. In the freezer aisle she stands too long in front of mint choc chip, then chooses vanilla because the world is loud and vanilla is quiet. At the register, the teen cashier stares at her eyes and fumbles the coins. Charlie pretends not to notice.

Back at Take Flight, shadows feel longer. Amelia drapes herself over Chase like armour he doesn't want, laughing too loud, claiming space that isn't hers. Emily catches my eye, shakes her head: don't let her in.

But later, I see Amelia drift toward Eli. He's behind the bar wiping down with a grin too easy, shoulders loose. She leans close, says something. He laughs, but it rings hollow. She presses a glass into his hand. He hesitates for a breath, then downs it.

Emily's jaw tightens. "That's how she works."

I watch Eli's grin dim as the alcohol goes down, his posture sagging like cut strings. Something knots in my stomach.

"She finds the cracks," Emily says. "Then she pries."

The words echo long after close.

Between rushes, a tray drops in the back and the crash detonates. Chase flinches. Not big—just a shoulder jerk and a look to the exits before he smooths it into nothing. Jesse clocks it and pretends he didn't. A long scar peeks under Chase's cuff when he lifts a crate; the skin there is a map of heat and shrapnel. Someone asks him—new barback, dumb courage—"That from, like, a motorbike?" Chase's mouth smiles with no teeth. "Something like that," he says, and moves on. Door closed, bolted.

At the back door I swing twice, hear the latch, palm-check steel. Still— the scrape from two nights ago crawls under my skin. Some cracks don't show until you stand still long enough to feel them.

Near midnight the front door huffs at the edge of closing time and a man stands half-in, half-out of rain as if undecided. He doesn't order. Doesn't cross the rubber mat. The jukebox throws a blue-green wash across his face and the rest of the room goes quiet in my head.

Green eyes that catch light like bottles. A hairline bolt of a scar over his brow.

I blink; a car splashes past. The door eases itself shut. No footprints on the mat. Only rain.

After cash-up, Jesse does the outside sweep. "Clear," he reports, but he stays ten extra seconds at the alley mouth like he's arguing with the shadows. When he comes back, he taps the frame twice—habit, spell, who knows.

"Go home," Emily orders gently. "Text when you're in."

"Bossy," I tell her.

"Manager," she corrects. She glances at her phone where a calendar ping glows—GP follow-up. Two hearts. She thumbs it away. "Tomorrow," she says, like a secret to herself.

On the tram, a woman with a cracked screen plays a video of someone's baby taking a first step. The whole carriage smiles like we practised. I send Charlie a dumb meme. She replies with a dragon emoji and a grainy photo of a page from the art room: doors, latches, a rabbit with a green ribbon.

At home, the building smells like dust and other people's dinners. I lock the door twice, then a third time after washing my face because I can't help it. Through the window, tail lights smear into commas. Somewhere a siren starts small and chooses distance.

On my pillow, sleep plays hard to get. When it finally comes, it brings a corridor with a lift-latch at hip height, a piano that bleeds ash, a woman with perfect nails whispering in a man's ear, and a hand at a door that isn't supposed to open from the outside.

I wake with my fists curled and the taste of metal at the back of my tongue.

Fault lines, I think. Everywhere.

And then I get up, tie my hair back, and

run.

Chapter Five:

The Door

Closing always feels longer than the night shift itself. The music dies, the crowd drains, and what's left is sticky floors, overturned glasses, and chairs balanced on tables like skeletons mid-dance.

Emily hums some pop song as she wipes counters, shoulders swaying as if this place doesn't still smell of sweat and spilled liquor. Jesse does his rounds with military precision: bathrooms checked, taps shut, exits tested. Eli leans too hard on the sink, polishing a clean glass, eyes glazed at the edges.

The checklist ticks down: mop, bottles, tills, spouts soaking. My hands are shaky but practiced. Routine keeps me steady.

I balance a crate of empties against my hip, the edge biting into my ribs, and head down the service corridor. The light buzzes overhead, flicker-sick, painting everything jaundiced. The hum of the fridge fades behind me.

The back door looms at the end. Paint scuffed thin, latch temperamental. Emily's voice runs through my head: Swing twice. Hear the latch. Check the latch. I did. I always do.

Still—my chest tightens as I set the crate down.

The handle rattles.

Sharp. Deliberate.

Not the usual stick. Not the wind. A hand. Testing.

My breath knots tight in my throat.

"Hello?" The word scrapes out too thin, too small.

Silence.

Then a scrape. Metal on metal. Slow. Patient. Like a key that doesn't belong trying its luck.

The crate slips from my grip. Bottles clatter, glass chiming against concrete.

"Cas?" Jesse's voice booms, steady, already moving.

I spin toward him, pulse thunder in my ears. "Someone—at the door—"

He's there before I finish, calm as a storm you didn't see coming. He throws the bar, swings the door wide.

Cold night crashes in. The alley yawns back at us: bins crouched against brick, shadows stretching, a bottle rolling lazy into the gutter. Nothing. No one. The air smells like rain-wet bitumen and damp cardboard; copper flickers in my mouth and won't leave.

Emily jogs up, torch in hand, hair escaping her knot. The beam slices the dark, checks the bins, finds only scraps and rats. Her eyes whip to me. Concern, not dismissal. "You, okay?"

I nod because words would split me open. My throat is too tight.

Chase arrives last, tie off, sleeves rolled, shadows under his eyes. He takes in the scene—door wide, Jesse steady, Emily tense, me shaking with glass shards at my feet.

"Locked?" he asks Jesse.

"Yeah. Still is."

Chase doesn't trust it. He tests the handle himself, swings it twice, listens for the latch, presses his palm flat to the cold steel. The silence stretches. Finally, he looks at me.

"We'll get a locksmith," he says, quiet but certain. "Tomorrow."

Emily snorts, sharp. "You've been saying tomorrow for weeks."

He ignores her, gaze steady on me. He doesn't say you're safe now. He doesn't say it's nothing. He just offers rope.

"If it sticks again," he says, low enough only I hear, "you call me. Doesn't matter the time. Don't check it alone. Got it?"

My voice is paper. "Got it."

The night limps on. Chairs stacked. Float counted. The jukebox sighs one last ghostly note before shutting down.

Eli fumbles his keys at the staff hook, misses twice. Jesse plucks them from his hand and taps his phone for a rideshare. "I'll watch the pin," he says. Eli's grin slants, brave and brittle. "I'm fine."

By the time I ride the tram home, my reflection in the window looks older than twenty-three. Jaw locked, eyes too wide, hair frizzed by kitchen steam.

At the apartment, Charlie is curled on the couch, textbook open across her chest like she fell asleep mid-sentence. I tuck a blanket around her. She doesn't stir.

In the bathroom, steam fogs the mirror until my reflection swims. Water needles my shoulders red, but when I close my eyes, I still hear it: the scrape of metal on metal. The patient rattle of someone who wasn't supposed to be there.

I press my fists to the tiles until my arms ache. "Get stronger," I whisper to the fog.

But the girl in the glass doesn't look

convinced.

Chapter Six

Triplet Falls Has Everyone Falling

Out past the ranges the air tastes like eucalyptus and rain that keeps changing its mind. Emily's hatchback coughs into the gravel car park at Triplet Falls and dies with an operatic wheeze. She spins in the seat, grin bright enough to startle birds.

"Ready to become one with nature?" she asks.

"I am nature," I deadpan, lacing boots. "You're the one who thinks a fern is a personality."

"Rude." She steps out and immediately skates on the damp verge, arms windmilling.

Jesse is there before gravity closes the sale, hand on her elbow, grin he tries and fails to hide.

"Did not fall," she declares.

"You descended with flair," he says.

Chase climbs out of the second car. No suit tonight—cargo pants, trail runners, windbreaker over a washed-grey tee. The sleeves are still pushed up, scars pale as old lightning. He catches me looking and holds the glance a second too long before looking away, like he's the one who owes an apology.

A kookaburra laughs from the treeline like it knows the punchline already. We shoulder packs and take the trail.

The first stretch is leaf litter and slick roots. The forest casts cold shade over our backs; birds riffle the canopy like gossip. Emily narrates every near-slip with theatrical outrage. Jesse walks behind her, not-subtly admiring the view while pretending to be about safety. I lead and let rhythm take the edge off city noise. Chase keeps pace beside me, gait evening out on flats, going careful on angles—bones that healed still remembering.

"You okay?" I ask, not looking over.

"Always," he says. A lie we both sign for today.

The track tips toward the first falls. Water throws itself over rock, white and furious. Mist beads our hair. Emily exhales. "Okay. Worth it."

We stand shoulder to shoulder at the wire fence and watch sunlight cut the spray into falling confetti. Talking is unnecessary. The roar eats our loud and leaves smallness. Relief.

Emily nudges me, conspiratorial. "Mind him coming?"

I glance at Chase. He's squinting into the mist, fingers unconsciously covering the thin seam at his wrist like water could read him.

"It's fine," I say. "He drinks water now. Civilised."

He huffs a laugh. Tension breaks. We push on.

The stairs to the second cascade make promises about your calves you didn't want. Chase slows a notch, not complaining, measuring each tread. Jesse hangs back with Emily like a bodyguard with a crush.

"Just in case you roll backwards," he says, palms hovering.

"Workplace safety," she deadpans.

We eat between the second and third falls on a patch of fence warmed by a shaft of sun. From our packs: ham-and-cheese rolls, fruit, biscuits with bright orange cheese dip, pop-tops that taste like childhood. We share crumbs and a quiet that doesn't need permission.

"Truth game," Emily announces suddenly. "Everyone gets a question."

"Oh no," Jesse groans.

"Too late." She points at me. "First crush."

"Year four," I say. "Boy who cried when he got a gold star. My type has always been emotionally literate."

"Lies," she chirps, delighted. Swivels to Jesse. "Worst job?"

"Mall-Santa security. Kids are fast. Parents are worse." He grimaces. "A small person bit me."

"On brand," Chase murmurs, mouth almost smiling.

Emily's gaze lands on him and stays. "Okay, your turn. Why Amelia?"

The sunlight tilts. Chase's jaw works. He unwraps a napkin with surgeon focus. "Next."

"No," she says softly, blade under velvet. "Answer."

He breathes in through his nose. "Because people like Amelia don't need me to be anything I can't be."

Emily's eyebrow climbs. "In English?"

"It means she doesn't look at me like a before-and-after photo," he says, the control fraying. "Like I'm a cautionary tale with a bank account. She wants what she wants and doesn't ask for more." He swallows.

"Efficient."

"Efficient," Emily repeats, disgust curling the edges. "So a woman who treats you like a trophy cabinet is safer than anyone who actually sees you?"

His temper flares like a match. "Who would? Be serious. This—" he gestures to the territory he protects with shirts and patience "—is not happy-ever-after material. It's a compromise people make because they like the piano and the money and the story of being kind."

"Stop," I say before the next words draw blood. He turns like he'd forgotten I was there. For a beat, his face is unarmoured.

"You don't get to decide what people can bear," I tell him, steady. "You don't get to put that in their mouths and call it truth."

He laughs without humour. "You'd turn away."

Heat spikes—anger at his certainty, at my sudden stupid desire to prove him wrong. "Don't think for me," I snap. "You know nothing about what I'd do."

Silence pops our little circle. Even the water seems to hold its breath.

"Break's over," Emily says too brightly, clapping once like a stage manager. "Stairs call."

We shoulder packs. Truce by movement. Walking gives our hands somewhere to be besides fists.

The third falls ambush us—trees part, the tiers appear, white water folding itself again and again into a dark pool. Tourists herd up with phones, all of us trying to trap a living thing in rectangles.

A man with a camera offers a photo. We line up normal first, arms around shoulders, smiles trying too hard. "One more," he says. "Something fun."

Emily launches onto Jesse's back without warning. He oofs, then steadies her thighs and does not complain. Chase glances at me, almost-smile. "We copy?"

"We copy," I say, and my body betrays me—up on his back, hands around his shoulders. He's stronger than he lets on. He straightens smoothly, heat shock through my palms. For a heartbeat my chin is at his ear, his breath in my hair, and the world narrows to balance, trust, not falling. The old seatbelt arc above my collarbone twinges—impact remembered, aborted. I breathe until the ache lets go.

Shutter. We disentangle with laughter and too many hands. The stranger shows us the shots. In the silly one, Emily's head is thrown back with unguarded joy; Jesse looks at her like he swallowed the sun; Chase's hands brace my calves as if I might levitate; I'm mid-laugh, unposed, alive.

We thank him and turn for the climb. The stairs look steeper in reverse. I step to crack a joke and miss the edge.

It's only two steps but my body chooses cliff—stomach gone, air gone, the old sick lurch of I'm about to hit.

Hands catch my waist. Haul me upright. Breath rough at my ear.

Chase is closer than people are supposed to be. His pupils are too wide. Mine, maybe worse. The forest contracts to pulse-in-throat and the heat of his fingers through fabric.

"You okay?" low enough wind has to lean in.

I nod. It's a truth and a lie. He lets go slowly, as if gravity is untrustworthy. I thank him with a crooked smile and suddenly need sky and a car and motion.

On the way back, a tradie-looking guy in a tour group lifts his head; the sun hits his eyes bottle-green. My muscles coil. Then he laughs and the laugh reaches both eyes. Wrong man. The line above his brow is time, not a scar. I let go of the breath I'd hoarded.

At the top we shake off awkward like mist. Emily hooks her arm through mine.

"Triplet Falls: everyone falling," she stage-whispers. "Not just the stairs."

I bump her with my hip. "You stayed upright all day. Miracle."

Back at the cars, the light goes honey-old. We pass the last of the water bottles around. Chase drifts over, hands in pockets, shoulders apologetic.

"Thanks for letting me come," he says.

"You invited yourself," I say too fast, then soften. "I'm glad you did."

Something in his face eases. He lifts a hand like he might touch my shoulder and thinks better of it.

"Home, children," Emily whistles, rescuing us both.

The drive back tastes like salt chips and quiet. The city grows out of the dark, a brand-new animal again.

We duck into Take Flight to stash gear and say goodnight. The falls photo pings the group chat before my phone finds the Wi-Fi. Emily captions it: **Team Grace. 10/10 would hike again.** A blue heart lands a beat later—Chase. I stare too long at a tiny icon and turn my phone face-down.

The door swings at the worst moment. Perfume, heels, glint. Amelia. She clocks the burrs on Emily's socks, mud on our boots, damp line at my waistband where mist got ambitious. Her smile could split an atom.

"Well," she purrs to Chase. "You kept them alive. How outdoorsy of you."

"Even packed snacks," Emily chirps. "Want one?" She offers a squashed roll like a treaty. Amelia doesn't look.

Her gaze flicks to me and narrows. "Cute photo," she says. "Very… trust-fall."

"We were near actual falls," I say, neutral.

"So literal." She laughs lightly, then rotates her body a degree to box me out and tilts her face to Chase. "Drink?"

"Water," he says.

"Boring." Her attention slides to Eli, stacking pints, a little loose at the edges, smile too eager. "You'll be fun, won't you?"

"I'm on shift," he says, soft. Not a no.

"One won't kill you." She nests a shot glass inside another with magician neatness. "Double for catching up. Chop-chop."

"Amelia," Emily warns, voice thin as wire.

"What? Hospitality." Amelia's lips curve; her eyes don't. She nudges the glass toward Eli's fingers. "To bravery."

He hates failing tests. He throws it back. His grin flickers, then drops a watt.

"Another?" she says, already tipping the bottle.

Emily's smile shows teeth as she plucks it away. "We're closed."

"I'm family," Amelia says.

"Family doesn't get staff fired," Jesse replies, appearing like weather again.

Amelia's gaze lands on me one last time, sugar crystallised to glass. "Careful on the stairs, Cas," she murmurs. "Long way down when no one's catching you."

She drifts off, perfume and the faintest hairline crack. Eli rubs his mouth like he's trying to press himself back into a better shape. Emily sets water in front of him and taps the bar twice. Drink. He obeys—for now.

By the time I get home, Charlie is waiting on the couch, arms folded like armour, eyes knife-sharp.

"Who's he?" she says, before hello.

"A friend," I say, unlacing boots. "And my boss."

Her gaze ticks to the scuff on my knee, the damp seam at my shirt hem. "You're smiling."

"I tripped. Someone caught me." I try for joke and land near confession. "Nothing will happen," I add, too quick—promise to her, warning to myself.

She snorts. "You say that like it's up to you." But when I kiss her forehead, she leans in. A truce.

In the shower, waterfall noise becomes water again. Close my eyes: his hands at my waist when I fell—terror, certainty, something reckless. Underneath: Amelia's neat smile, sharpened. I turn the tap hotter until my skin insists on honesty.

I am not a project. I am not a cure. He is not a monster. Amelia isn't a storm; she's the humidity that makes everything combustible. None of this is simple. The trick is to move without bolting.

In bed, the photo pings again. Jesse reacts with fire emojis because he is a teenage boy in a very large body. Chase adds nothing else. I stare at the small blue heart, turn the phone

face-down, and ask the room to stay quiet.

Tomorrow can be about routine. Tonight,

I'll settle for the memory of not falling.

Keep Being Scared or Start Fighting Back

Closing shift is muscle memory now. Chairs on tables. Floors mopped until the sticky patch by the cider tap finally surrenders. Till counted, glasses racked, music cut. The jukebox wheezes one last ghost note and dies.

After hours, the bar is too quiet. Silence presses like a palm over my mouth. I hum off-key while I stack mats, just to keep sound moving. It's dumb—Chase would roast me for killing the soundtrack before the last lock—but silence gnaws worse.

Eli leans on the sink, polishing a glass already clean. Edges glazed, a smile he can't stand behind. Perfume clings to the varnish— a cheap, sweet fog that doesn't belong to anyone who loves this place.

Emily slides him water. "Drink."

"I'm fine," Eli says, slipperiest word I know.

"Drink," Jesse repeats, softer and somehow heavier. Eli obeys. For now.

The latch gives a wrong click.

I don't notice the door until the air changes shape with a new presence.

Then he's in.

Black shape. Mask. Knife that catches the fluoro and throws it back cold. Breath wet through wool, a small whistle on the exhale.

The sound that exits me isn't a scream. It's an edge sucked in—sharp and too small to hold anything.

He's on me before my brain finishes the sentence. Fist in my ponytail, head yanked back so hard stars ring the ceiling. The pull tears at the scalp, lightning in the roots. The knife kisses my throat—a thin, metallic promise.

Air stops. My lungs turn to fists.

He murmurs filth that isn't language but knows how to be humiliation. Not a robbery. He didn't come for the till.

Metal talks when he moves. Each shift drags the blade and breath becomes fire. His weight pins me to the bar; my old seatbelt scar—the X above my collarbone—flares hot, a cross burning under skin. A memory of restraint. A prayer that once worked.

I think of Charlie. Just Charlie. Her head under my arm in a hospital corridor. Her dragons in the margins. Her counting of breathable seconds.

Pain blooms in waves that overlap until time is only hurt. Pins and needles race up my forearms; fingers go dumb. He laughs when he feels the tremor—small and cheerful, like a kid finding a toy. The knife snicks sideways and opens heat along my ribs.

He wants me folded. He wants me quiet. Something in me refuses.

I buck and slam the back of my skull into his nose. A crunch like someone stepping onto thin ice. He yelps—surprise more than pain—and his grip stutters. Air floods in raw and furious.

Run.

Clothes tangled at my ankles, blood slick at my side, I lunge for my phone. He catches my arm; the knife scores a red smile under my ribs. Heat whites out the edges. I stamp the arch of his foot. He curses—wet, animal—and I tear free.

The stairs. The office. Alarm.

I take them wrong—knees then hands.
My body is an animal that knows only up.

His hand hooks my ankle; he drags me
down a step, another. Knife kisses thigh,
hotter this time. I kick blind and meet shin. He
swears, a cracked-tooth sound.

I tumble into the office and slam the door.
Turn the lock. My body shakes too hard to
balance on bones alone. Blood slicks the
keypad. I wipe my fingers on my shirt and jab
the code. Silent alarm. One minute. Forever
and not enough.

He hits the door. The frame shudders.
Vibrations travel through drywall and spine. I
can taste the screws.

There's a window. Two floors to
concrete. Not survivable. Not today.

I scrabble for weight. My palm closes around a brass bookend shaped like an ampersand. Heavy. Cold. *And.* I crouch behind the hinge side and whisper Charlie's name into my teeth like it can arrest time.

The lock gives. Steel slams into me; my shoulder pops bright. I bring the bookend up. He steps in, knife high, eyes inside the mask—green glass and a thin lightning nick above the brow. I will know that scar in a fractured mirror. I will know those eyes in the dark.

"Drop it!" Jesse's voice, big enough to bend walls.

Light floods—torches, the alley's red-blue stutter. The alarm shows its teeth.

"On the ground!" another voice, trained to be gravity.

The knife wavers. His eyes flick to the hall, to me, back. He chooses forward.

Chase takes him out of the air. They hit the rail; wood decides splinters are simpler. The knife flashes and reappears near Jesse's belly; Jesse twists but not fast enough. The blade bites. Blood jumps like it's glad to be free.

The intruder uses the angle and is gone— down the stairs, past the wrong blue uniforms, into the night that loves a secret.

I'm left in a triangle of light and noises and the heavy & cutting a crescent into my palm.

Chase is first to me. His jacket becomes a blanket I didn't consent to but need. He lifts me like I weigh nothing and I let him because my legs have elected to be water. Sirens and voices smear into streaks outside the door. Jesse's hand is a clamp over his own red mouth; Emily is ice-white and furious, saying his name like she's telling it to stay.

Hospital light is honest, not kind. Machines keep count. Bandages net my ribs and thigh into a new geometry—lattice to force a shape. Every breath filets itself. The X above my collarbone throbs like a lit cross: you are still here.

"Charlie's safe," Chase says when I thrash for a name. "Emily's with her. She doesn't know details."

A sob breaks free and keeps going. I shake so hard the rails complain. Chase covers my hand and anchors without squeezing. Jesse stands in the corner with a fresh dressing like an insult; Emily is attached to him by gravity and will.

Detectives bring clipboards and apologies. Questions snag and slide. A camera flashes; I flinch like it's a hand. Swabs. Photographs. Nail scrapings. Questions about older scars. My body is evidence; my voice is suspect. Shame crawls up my neck; fury snaps at its heels.

A woman with ballast in her step waits last. **Noor**. Her voice is steady without cotton. "Cassianna," she says, like the name belongs to me, not the report. "We'll go at your pace."

She leaves the silences intact so I can sit down in them. When words won't come, she hands me water like she's passing time itself and lets me drink both.

"Whoever did this wants you smaller," she says finally. "That's not the story I'm writing." I don't believe her yet. I like that she says it.

Morning is worse and a little better. Charlie arrives raw-edged and folds herself under my arm so carefully I cry again. She doesn't ask for the story. She listens to my pulse and decides it's enough.

Interlude – A Week That Eats Itself

Home is not home. It is a corridor with too many doors.

On night one, I sleep in five-minute segments like a broken metronome. Every creak is a boot on the landing. The fridge breath is a man's breath through wool. I lock the front door twice, then a third time, then count to a hundred and do it again.

On night two, sleep paralysis finds me. I wake to the weight of someone sitting on my sternum, pressure like a stone on a grave. I can't move. The room hums in a single flat line. Eyes open, I'm a pinned insect. In the doorway, a man stands—negative space wearing shoulders—glass-green eyes and that bolt of a brow. I try to scream and swallow it. When my body finally lets go, I tumble out of the bed and vomit into a towel I don't remember grabbing. My hair knots with sweat; I don't wash it. I don't wash anything.

By day three, I don't leave my room. The world is outside and that's where knives come from. The mirror has a towel over it because my face in glass looks like a stranger who can't be trusted not to open the door. I listen to the building: tap-drip, lift whine, neighbour laugh. Every sound has teeth. Every silence is worse.

On day four, Emily sits on the hall carpet and speaks to the closed door like it's me. "Tea on the mat," she says. "Toast. I'm not going anywhere." I hear the soft friction of her jeans as she slides down the wall and hums off-key. Later, the cup is empty and I don't remember drinking it.

Night terrors come like trains: I wake mid-scream, heart doing hummingbird, fists bruising my own thighs because my body is trying to get out of itself. Charlie's voice through the wood is too young: "Cas?" I tell her I'm fine through a mouth full of tin. She's not stupid. I hear her crying into a pillow she thinks is a secret.

On day five, I try the shower. The water stings the cuts until they sing. I scrub my skin with cheap lemon dish soap until the bathroom smells like Mum's hands and I shake so hard I have to sit on the floor. My hair mats in ropes; the comb catches and my scalp screams and I give up. The X at my collarbone burns like someone lit it from below.

That night I hear the scrape again—metal on metal, patient as a metronome. I know it's memory. I know it. My body doesn't. Panic detonates. Vision tunnels. Hands go pins, then numb. The world folds at the edges; the room leans to one side. I claw the carpet because it feels like falling and I need to hold something.

Charlie finds me on my knees between bed and wall, sobbing air that won't come. She freezes. The fear on her face is a mirror I can't stand. She fumbles the phone; it rattles against the jamb.

Emily gets there first, voice steady, breath louder on purpose. She stays low, a body making a smaller horizon. "With me, Cas. Look at me. Four in." She holds up fingers. "One—two—three—four. Good. Six out. One—two—three—four—five—six."

She counts me a rope across a river. She doesn't touch me until I nod. When she does, it's the back of my hand, not my wrist. Her palm is a place to balance the air.

Chase fills the doorway behind her, too big for the room, trying to fold himself smaller. He narrates his nearness like a treaty. "Left of the door," he says. "Not coming close." His voice is a deeper metronome under Emily's.

Charlie stands at the foot of the bed, arms wrapped around herself like she's trying to hold her pieces together. She has never looked afraid of me. Now she is. I want to claw my own throat open and take the sound back.

The worst of it passes like a storm that was always going to pass, too slow to feel like a mercy. When I can breathe without lying,

Emily tucks hair—knotted and sour—behind my ear and says, "We're going to make a plan that you own. Not the fear."

Chase says nothing useful and nothing wrong. He watches the door like he can will it to be an unbreakable species. When he finally speaks, it's only: "Do you want me to stand outside tonight?" It is the smallest question and the biggest relief. I nod. He goes.

On day six I try the hall. It's too long. The light at the end is interrogation. I take three steps and retreat, heart in my mouth, bile in my throat. I cut a T-shirt into strips and braid my hair so it stops catching on everything. It looks like a nest someone died in. I leave it that way.

On day seven I write my resignation. Three sentences. Thank you. Sorry. I can't come back. The letters don't look like mine.

My hand shakes and the pen leaves a spray of

dots I don't bother to fix. I put the envelope in

my bag and sit on the bed until the window

goes from grey to silver to black.

I believe my life has been stolen. My

safety is a story other people get to tell.

Everything creaks. Even when it doesn't, I

hear it.

When I stand, my legs remember old

math. I put one foot in front of the other until

the tram arrives to carry me to the act of

disappearing.

Charlie's POV — Glass Wings

Hospitals turn breath into rules: in

through your nose, out through your mouth.

Sit. Don't block the corridor. Don't touch the

machines that pretend they're not listening. Be brave when no one has told you how.

Emily bought me a hot chocolate that grew a skin while nobody looked. I blew it sideways and drank anyway because adults are calmer when you use cups for the job they were given. Jesse sat across with a bandage smiling through his shirt and told a story about a cat that had mauled him worse. It was a lie with good intentions. I liked it.

They asked if I wanted to go home and wait. Home is too loud with not-knowing. I said no.

I drew because drawing makes time behave. On one page, the bar floor. I turned glass into triangles with light caught in them and taped them to a girl's shoulder blades so she could leave a room that didn't have a door in the right place.

When they let me in, Cas was a map of roads closed after rain. I climbed onto the bed and fit myself under her arm, careful around the tape and thread and new geometry. She flinched and said sorry, which is ridiculous. I tucked my ear under the place where her ribs and the machine talked until they agreed.

A social worker with a cardigan and a mouth made for kind orders said words in a soft arrangement. Guardian landed in the middle and refused to move. I didn't look at it. You can ignore a word for a long time if you stare at your sister's knuckles instead.

Later she woke up shaking and the room tried to be the right shape and kept almost making it. "She was screaming," I said, and hated that my voice cracked like a plate you liked. Emily rocked her like small children get rocked. Jesse leaned on paint and tried to hold it up. Chase stood at the end of the bed like a door practicing being a shield.

When Cas slept again I pressed a finger to the old half-moon at her collarbone—a seatbelt bruise that did its job—and wished for a kind of seatbelt you could wear at night.

On the way back I stuck my drawing on the staff noticeboard with blue tack stolen from a hand-hygiene sign. A nurse said, "Nice wings." I said, "They're for flying away." She said, "Or for staying." I didn't know wings could be used both ways. I put that in a pocket to learn later.

In the vending machine reflection, a woman in a dark coat walked past with a phone to her ear. Her eyes slid away when she heard Eli's name at the nurses' station. I added that to the other pocket where numbers and names and the shape of things go when they're not ready to be solved.

Chapter Eight:

Bitesize

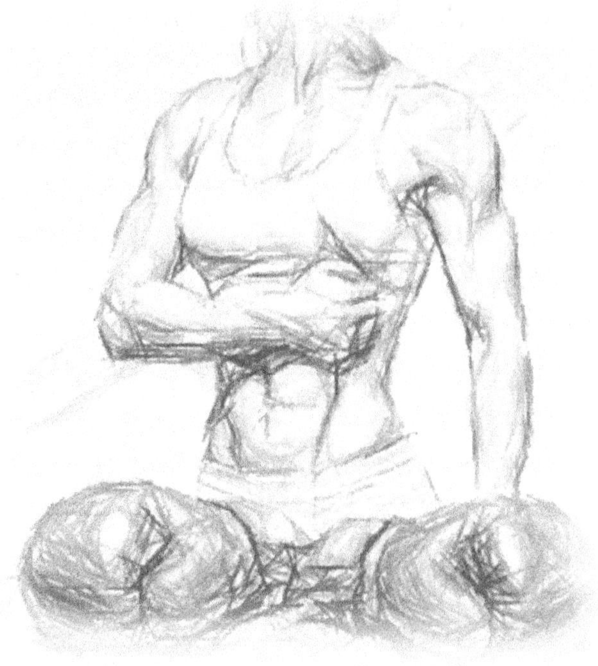

My resignation sits on Chase's desk like a dare I meant to win. He steps into the doorway and refuses to read it out loud, and the small hard part of me that hasn't died yet sits up straight.

"Keep being scared," he says in a voice built for orders and apologies, "or start fighting back."

The choice echoes down the corridor as I push through the stairwell door. Dust floats in the beam like slow snow. Beneath the steps, a storage door gapes. I hesitate. If I don't move now, I won't. So I move.

The room smells like canvas and rubber and a kind of clean that is earned. The metal stairs ring underfoot. It should not exist here, a bright space tucked under a bar like a secret backbone. A ring waits in the centre, roped and square as a promise. Heavy bags hang like quiet men. Pads, wraps, gloves. A towel folded like a chapel cloth.

"What changed your mind?" he asks, silencing his phone and pocketing it like he's tucking away a persona.

"Charlie," I say. It's the only true answer that fits. "I can't run and keep her safe at the same time."

He nods like he was waiting for that sentence. He lifts red hand wraps and crooks a finger. "Hands."

I give them before fear remembers its lines. He wraps with practice: anchor at the wrist; across the palm; catch the thumb; figure-eight bones into a team. His fingers are warm through gauze. He narrates what he's doing like an instructor who knows surprise is a weapon. He steps back as soon as the knot lies flat.

"Stance." Tap. "Here. Shoulder width. Knees soft. Chin tucked. Hands up. Breathe."

I breathe. Not like a poster. Like someone learning a new instrument. In for four. Out for six. Numbers I can actually hold.

He edges a bag toward me with the easy, crooked strength of a man who lives in his body like renters live—never fully owning, always aware of the walls. "Jab. Straight line. Turn the hip. Exhale on contact."

I throw the jab and my wrist buckles. Pain shoots up my forearm like an unhelpful friend. Shame arrives behind it, late and loud.

"Good start," he says as if I didn't nearly fold. He resets my fist, nudges my elbow, taps my shoulder. "Don't swing. Push. Again."

Thunk instead of slap. The bag answers like it noticed me. In that small, ridiculous sound something shifts. An inch of floor belongs to me.

"Cross," he says. "Same idea on the power side. Show your shoulder where to go."

I throw the cross. The bag rocks in acknowledgment. A laugh barks out of me, feral and wet. He grins, quick and surprised, like we both forgot laughter is a thing.

"Bitesize," he says. "You take it one piece at a time. That's how you win."

The word lands like a name you didn't know you were waiting for. It means I don't have to lift the building at once. Just a brick. Then another.

Hooks. Uppercuts. Steps that teach my bones a new alphabet. Sweat runs down my spine. Stitches argue at my ribs. He sees the flinch I try to bury; the way my shoulders go glass when his shadow crosses. He never enters my blind side. *Right side,* he says. *Fixing your wrist. Behind you now.* Touch paired with sentence. Consent in syntax.

It is work to be touched in daylight, but here the work has rules.

We finish with knees. "For no-space," he says, pad strapped across his stomach. "When they're already too close."

Too close. The pad narrows into the knife. The rope becomes a corridor. The air sharpens to wool and metal and the wrong sound of breath. My skin floods with old heat.

He drops the pad and lifts his hands away. "Cas," he says, soft but unwilling to break. "We stop here."

"I'm okay," I lie like I want it to be true. "I can do it."

"We stop here," he repeats, kindness refusing to move. "You came down. You hit the bag. You found your stance. That's enough."

Enough is a word I don't trust. My legs are water. My hands vibrate inside red wraps like the wraps are holding bees. I nod.

He unwinds me. The ribbon falls into his palm. He doesn't comment on the tremor or the way the tiny bones click back toward normal. He folds the fabric and sets it down like a thing with value.

"You'll be sore," he says. "Hot shower. Water. Salt. Tomorrow, you'll be angry at me."

"I'm already not mad," I say, and hear the truth of it.

Upstairs, the bar's daytime breath: Emily's quick laugh, Jesse's low weather, clink of glass. Heels tap at the rail. "Baaabe," Amelia sings in that voice that makes everything into a performance. "You disappearing again?"

Chase's jaw sets; I can feel him put his costume on. "Session's done," he calls. "Five."

Amelia peers down the stairwell like a cat into a vent. Her gaze slides over me like a barcode scanner. "Sweating in secret?" she says. "Cute. Thought you'd pick a girl who can swing, Chase."

He doesn't bite. "See you upstairs."

She leaves perfume that makes the air taste like plastic fruit. I swallow the sentence that would flame the room for no gain.

"I'll walk you out," he says.

"I'm fine."

"I know." He holds the side door anyway. It isn't chivalry. It's a contingency he can control.

Outside, the air tastes like rain about to keep a promise. He doesn't say *call if.* He already did. He doesn't say *safe* because he won't lay hands on a word he can't deliver. He says, "Tomorrow. If you want."

"Tomorrow," I say, and the word lands like a rung.

On the tram I catalogue aches like inventory: wrists, shoulders, ribs. Pain I chose. Pain that is already teaching.

At home, Charlie is at the bench with a sketchbook and a mug that is mostly sugar holding cocoa hostage. "How was it?" she asks, wariness and hope in the same exhale.

"Hard," I say. "Good."

She closes the book as if it's secret, but I see enough: glass shards repurposed into wings; a green ribbon threaded through the hinge like a spine. "Taylor said my eyes are pretty," she blurts. "Like rare-pretty. Not creepy."

"That's because they are," I say, bumping her hip. "Rare-pretty sounds like a bird we haven't discovered."

She rolls her eyes but the smile is real. When she hugs me, my chest hurts in the best way.

The shower finds new bruises blooming like midnight flowers. I lay a palm over the thickest line of stitches and count until the sting softens. *Bitesize.* One thing. Then another.

After, I scrub my hands with the cheap lemon dish soap. The smell chases gym and wool and metal off my skin—for a minute. That's all I need.

Sleep comes cleaner. A piano chord that doesn't hurt. A rabbit with a green ribbon sitting precisely where the ache used to live.

And under it all, the cross at my collarbone burns like a small, lit truth: I am not done.

Interlude — Seven Years Ago (Cas, 16)

Sam wore the kind of smile teachers call potential and mothers call trouble. He wore it like a jacket he hadn't learned how to take off. We met by the bus bay in summer when the tar went soft and tried to keep you. He said I looked like I knew where I was going. I didn't. He followed anyway.

When I was late, Mum would say my name like a bell—*Cassianna*—and then say it again to make the day behave. The night I told her, she said it like a prayer with a knot in it.

The clinic smelled like lemons pretending to be clean. A nurse with careful eyes wrote on a chart without looking at me. Sam squeezed my hand in the way people do when they're trying to make a bubble and take you inside it.

We made a plan that wasn't one: finish school, save money, love hard enough to make the rest true.

Plans are good until the road floods.

I laboured in a room whose window stared at a brick wall. Mum kept a cool cloth moving on my forehead as if motion was a spell. Dad stood like a tree you always thought would outlive you and suddenly understood could fall. Someone said push and I did and something ancient and brand-new arrived and screamed her opinion about air.

They put her on my chest for one breath. Small. Furious. Perfect. In my head I called her **Rosaleigh** because saying it out loud would make it easier to steal.

They lifted her to the other side where machines blinked like undecided gods. The nurse's mouth made a shape her eyes wouldn't follow. Mum said, *It's okay, duck,* the way she did when she didn't know if it would be.

Words came after: complications. not breathing. we're trying. I tried too—to stand up out of my body and go where she was— but hurt was a tide and the brick wall filled the world.

When I woke, the cot was empty and the room smelled like nothing. Dad sat with his face in his hands. Mum smoothed my hair and said, "She didn't make it." I believed her because I had been taught to. I grieved the way I knew how: thoroughly, quietly, like cleaning a kitchen after a party no one should have thrown.

Sam left before the mud dried. He said he couldn't breathe here. I said I understood and then I understood.

Weeks later, a form fell out of the discharge packet. Boxes and lines, a place for a name that was blank, a line that didn't fit: *Infant transferred.* A time. An unreadable scrawl. I asked Mum and she said clerical and her hands rattled the tea in the cup.

I put the form with the hospital bracelet and the picture where you can see the top of a tiny ear. Every year I wrote **R.** on the calendar and baked a cupcake and didn't eat it. I tied a green ribbon around the box because I needed something to hold onto that would hold back.

If I close my eyes I can feel her weight for that one breath. If I open them I can see the nurse who wanted to say a different sentence and could not find a doorway for it.

I didn't tell anyone for years. I learned to hold grief in my teeth like a coin and talk around it. When I finally said her name out loud, the world didn't end. It just admitted it had already changed.

Chapter Nine:

Glass Lessons

The ache is worse on waking. Knuckles throb. Ribs cinched with wire. But pain has edges I can lean against; I'm greedy for anything I can name.

Charlie hovers in the doorway with the awkwardness of a teenager deciding whether to be kind.

"You want tea?"

"Please." The word tastes strange—soft, unarmoured.

She returns with two mugs and tucks her feet under her like she's five again.

"Ms Patel liked my sketch," she says, casual as breathing. "Said I should come to art club. Thursdays."

"Do it," I say. "Obviously."

"It means I'll be late home once a week."

"Then you'll text me once a week, and I won't die." Blow on tea. "Deal?"

She snorts. "Deal."

When she leaves, I scroll past messages I can't answer yet. Condolences, call if you need anything, and an unknown number—missed call, no voicemail. A breath catches. Nothing and everything. I save it without a name and put the phone face-down like I've done something dangerous. Which, maybe, I have.

At **Take Flight**, afternoon is checklist monotony—cash drawers, delivery receipts, a supplier who insists the lime shortage is "global and personal." Emily fans herself with invoices.

"You're glowing," she says, peering over the

paper. "Exercise glow or our boss making you sweat?"

"Gross," I say, but I'm smiling. "Show me the afternoon close again."

She runs me through it and I love her for pretending I didn't almost die here. "Jesse's bodging a temporary latch out back," she adds. "Proper locksmith Wednesday."

"What's wrong with today?" slips out sharper than I mean.

"What's wrong is the waiting list," she says. "But Jesse's a wall. You're not walking to the tram alone regardless."

At five, Eli drifts in late, sunglasses indoors. He peels them off; his blink is two beats slow. "Traffic," he says, like that explains the stale whiskey.

Emily's mouth goes flat. "Breath mints. Water. Job."

He salutes and saunters. The saunter is off; his smile arrives before he does.

"Hey, Cas," he says behind the bar, grin nearly right, towel over one shoulder. "You good?"

"Better," I say—the closest to truth that fits a public place.

His gaze catches on the tape-scuffed knuckles. "Training with Chase?"

I brace for mockery and get curiosity. "Yeah."

"Good." His grin wobbles. "That's…good."

Amelia leans over the ice well, red lipstick half-mooning her straw. "Careful, Eli," she murmurs, not looking at me. "You know how he gets when his projects start walking."

The barb lands somewhere tender I didn't know was exposed. Eli's jaw ticks; he turns away too fast, like he's the one cut.

I find him in the storeroom later, counting stock and not counting at all.

"You, okay?" I ask.

He laughs. It scrapes. "You're the one who got carved at and still came back."

"That's not what I asked."

He shrugs. "Some of us are background characters, Cas. Easier when the plot twists hit."

"Don't talk about yourself like that." My mother's voice in my mouth. "You'd have no one left if you did."

He eyes me—amused, moved, ashamed.

"Since when are you the therapist?"

"Since I needed one."

He smiles for real. Small and sore, like a blister forming. "Get out of here with your logic."

We both laugh, quietly, like we're not sure it's allowed.

After close, Chase catches me in the corridor and juts his chin toward the hidden room.

"You up for it, Bitesize?"

"I'm sore."

"That's not an answer."

"I'm up for it," I admit.

Jab. Cross. Hook. His patience is infuriating and perfect. No empty praise; each "good" is a brick. Footwork—quiet steps, small pivots—lines on the mat I'm learning to own. In for four, out for six. 1–5–1 until my hands remember.

"Again," he says when I think I'm done. "Last round."

I want to tell him no; I set my feet instead and drive a cross that smacks the bag hard enough to sting. I'm grinning before I realise.

He's grinning too. "That's the one."

We climb to Cupid's Wing because he asks if I want silence or a song and I surprise us both by saying "play." He lifts the lid like he's greeting a shy animal and coaxes a melody that threads rain up glass. For three minutes my ribs forget to ache.

The front door shoulder-checks open. Perfume. A laugh like a slap.

Amelia with two glossy friends. She clocks the piano, him, me; files it all.

"Rehearsal, darling? Or serenade?"

"Soundcheck," he says, polite enough to be rude.

One friend wanders toward places rats walk; the other props at the bar. Amelia drapes a hand on the lid and looks at me like I'm a stain to identify.

"It takes resilience to keep coming back," she says. "I admire that in staff. Work ethic is rare."

"Boundary is rarer," I say, even.

Her eyes flash, then cool. "Sweetheart, I built this place before you knew which end of a shaker to hold."

"Then stop loosening the screws," Emily says from the doorway, voice bright as a blade. She must have been there the whole time. "We're shut till six, Amelia. Bring your charity case back later." A glance at the friend fingering the keg couplers. "You too, honey."

Amelia's smile cuts. "You do love a stray, Em."

"Yeah," Emily says. "I do."

For a breath, no one moves. Then Amelia steps back, palms up. "Relax. We're all family here."

"Then act like it," Jesse says, filling the hall like a shadow that works for us.

They go. The air they leave behind tastes cleaner.

Chase looks at me, apology half-formed. I shake my head—don't you dare—and mouth, again.

He plays. This time I sit. This time I listen to the last quiet note.

Before lockup, I swing the back door twice, hear the latch, lay my palm to cold metal. Solid. Emily taps a folded business card into the frame by the schedule—Detective Noor's—like a talisman. "Just in case," she says. "Cameras are finally behaving."

"Good," I say, and mean it.

At home, Charlie is at the table, pages full of fractured shapes that resolve if you stand back—wing, river, face.

"Ms Patel says my lines are 'decisive'," she reports.

"They are," I say, looking the way she wants me to—arm's length, and then close.

"You're building something that only looks broken up close."

She tilts her head. "Deep."

"I'm full of it. Don't tell your friends."

This time she doesn't roll her eyes. She just turns the page and keeps drawing, the green ribbon at her wrist flashing like a small flag that means keep going.

After she sleeps, I sit on the kitchen floor with Mum's baby blanket and find the tiny knot on the back where her stitching caught. I press my thumb there until it leaves a crescent.

The phone buzzes once on the counter. Unknown number. I let it ring out. It stops. I breathe and tell myself that not answering is also an answer.

Interlude — Detective Noor: Case Notes

Subject: CASSIANNA *Cas* [Redacted]

Incident: Aggravated assault (knife) at licensed premises

Notes: Subject presenting with acute PTSD: sleep paralysis, night terrors, hypervigilance, withdrawal. Sister (Charlie, 15) showing secondary trauma. Employer (Chase [Redacted]) providing informal support.

Plan: Incremental engagement. Empowerment frame ("not the story he's writing"). Establish continuity between police response and daily safety. Monitor unknown male contact ("Sam") and Amelia [Redacted] for relevance.

Noor: Case Note 7

Subject returned to workplace within two weeks of incident. Observable hypervigilance mitigated by supportive coworkers (Emily, Jesse). Unknown number in phone log—monitor. Reinforce grounding skills; avoid retraumatisation by minimising interviews. Next check-in scheduled.

Noor: Case Note 9

Eli [Redacted] showing signs of substance use. Amelia [Redacted] manipulative presence at bar. Cas displaying protective instincts toward staff; potential displacement of trauma. Continue observation.

Chapter Ten:

Fault Tolerance

Wednesday brings the locksmith who shakes his head at the swollen frame like it personally offended him. He swaps the bar, planes the edge, fits a second deadbolt. Jesse shadows him like a dog with questions and an eye for angles until the man finally says, "Mate, if someone wants in, they get in," which is simultaneously useless and true.

"Then we make it loud and slow," Jesse mutters. He tests the latch twice. Three times. Four. "And we make it cost them."

Chase stands back with his hands in his pockets, boss-calm, throwing money at a problem until it considers surrender. When the locksmith leaves, he runs the drill himself anyway—open, close, open, close—until the clunk is consistent, until the door behaves like a door and not a dare.

"Better?" he asks.

"Better," I admit, because lying to the people who keep you whole is a waste of air.

By evening, weekend swells forward like a tide. Amelia is everywhere, glitter at her throat catching light that isn't meant for her. She kisses Chase like a claim and watches me like a warning. Eli laughs at jokes that take two beats to reach him. Emily mothers with teeth. Jesse watches doors and men and the spaces between them.

Around midnight, football boys spill in—aftershave, loud vowels, wet shoes. One with a shovel jaw leans too far over the bar and calls me sweetheart in a voice that swims. The nearness flips my stomach like a coin.

Before I can plant a boundary, Jesse is there, big and calm. "Back off the rail, mate."

"We're friendly," the boy says, laying his hand over mine like he's testing the tensile strength of skin.

I step away. "Order or move aside."

He grins. "Order you." His friends whoop like seals.

Jesse's palm settles on the bar between us. "That's your one warning."

The boy weighs it—stupid and arrogant both—then slops his hand back with an exaggerated bow. "Ginny tonic, sweetheart." The wink is the kind you give a machine before you kick it.

I make it, because not every indignity deserves my everything. The glass talks when I slide it across.

"Nice," Emily says under her breath. "Want me to spit in the next one?"

"Don't waste the spit," I say, and mean it.

Break finds Eli at the edge of Cupid's Wing staring at the closed piano lid like it might answer back.

"You ever play?" I ask, to be kind.

He shrugs. "Used to. Before pouring drinks was my personality."

"Pouring drinks is an art," I say.

He rolls his eyes at the lie on purpose, which makes us both smile.

Amelia materialises like smoke. "Eliiiii," she sings. "I told Chase you'd cover tomorrow so we can check out that new place with the mirrors."

"We're fully staffed," he says, not looking at her. "I'm on."

"You're…flexible," she purrs, threat nestled in sugar. A crystal vial clinks against her bracelets; she palms a shot onto the ledge.

"Edge-smoother. On me."

He hesitates just long enough to lose the moment and knocks it back. His smile lands second. Something in me knots.

Interlude — Detective Noor: Case Note

Subject demonstrating increased assertiveness at bar; successful boundary with intoxicated patron. Amelia continues to exert influence on Eli. Consider welfare check. Unknown number reappeared; transcript pending.

Case: Take Flight Assault

Lead Detective: Noor Kamran

Status: Open

Subject: Cassianna [Redacted]

"Survivors live in numbers. Perpetrators live in shadows. My job is to move them out of the dark."

Photos, time stamps, stills from the under-door tool mark.

A grainy frame of a green ribbon on a girl's wrist in a mirror at the back of the bar.

Another of Amelia with a hand at Eli's elbow.

Her pencil scribbles beside each:

"Pattern?"

"Leverage?"

"Influence?"

In the margin, a line she never types into

a report:

She looks like she's already writing her own

closing statement. Give her a different ending.

Chapter Eleven:

Flight Path

I wake to sunlight slicing Charlie's blinds, brightness shocking after nights lit only by hospital fluorescents and dream-knives. For the first time in weeks, I've slept without jolting and counting the gaps between her breaths. My body aches, ribs strapped, but the morning feels softer. Possible.

Sugar and butter pull me to the kitchen. Charlie is at the stove, tongue out at the corner of her mouth as she flips French toast like it's a test she intends to ace. She dusts sugar, fans strawberries, pretends not to check that I'm watching.

"You're showing off," I say, voice gravel.

"Better than your burnt toast."

She's fifteen and already more adult than I want her to be. She sets two plates, precise, then sits like this is routine. Like she's the one taking care of me.

We eat until the silence is something friendly. I put my fork down. "Take the day off. Come with me."

Her brow goes defensive. "Why?"

"Because bullies don't get to make you small. And because I want to teach you what Chase is teaching me. Self-defence."

She stares, suspicious, then smirks. "So… sister fight club?"

"Something like that."

Maybe she wants a break from the girls who sneer at her eyes. Maybe she sees through me and knows I need her in the room. Either way, we pack gym clothes and head to Take Flight.

Emily is bright at the bar, though her eyes snag on my bruises and stay too long. "She's really coming?" she asks, chin at Charlie.

"She's tougher than me," I say.

"Low bar," Jesse rumbles from his post.

Chase appears with a towel around his neck. Amelia trails behind in stilettos and a dress you shouldn't wear near mats. Her gaze takes in me, then Charlie, blade-sharp. "Sweat is disgusting," she mutters, like prayer.

Charlie snorts loud enough to carry. I nudge her, failing to hide my grin.

We pair up. Emily with Jesse, natural orbit. Chase volunteers with Charlie, which earns him a sceptic once-over before she shrugs and gloves up. That leaves me with Eli.

At first, it's almost normal. Gloves up, pads ready. The smell of canvas and rubber.

My phone alarm buzzes from the bench—
same pitch as a hospital monitor—and the
room tilts. Edges glitter. By the time I drag
my focus back, Eli's jab lands flush.

My head snaps; stars bite. I stagger,
shocked.

Everything stops. Charlie drops her
gloves and rushes me. Chase is right behind,
voice razor. "Are you kidding me?"

"I'm fine," I manage, lip stinging. "I
dropped my guard. My fault."

Chase crouches, fingers at my chin,
tilting left-right, checking like he has the
right. I lower his hand, flat. "I said I'm fine."

Eli's apology is immediate and paper-
thin. His hands shake. Behind him, Amelia
perches on the stairs, filing her nails. Her

laugh is quiet and mean every time someone stumbles.

"My round," I say, strapping tighter, forcing lightness into my voice. "He owes me."

I touch the old seatbelt arc above my collarbone and count. In 1-2-3-4. Out 1-2-3-4-5-6. 1–5–1 until my hands listen. Eli keeps his punches on the pads like a penitent writing line. When we finish, he hugs the wall like it will hold him up.

Chase takes Charlie onto the mitts. "Hands up, kid. Feet light. Eyes on me."

"My eyes are always on," she says, half-dare.

"I know," he says, and means it. He shows her how to slip, how to push rather than swing, how to breathe. She learns fast because she's been dodging since kindergarten. When Amelia scoffs, Charlie throws two clean jabs that crack the mitt sweet, then looks over and smiles like a girl who just discovered her own teeth. A small, bright thing unfurls in my chest.

We finish on the mats, breath tangled. Emily tosses me a towel; Jesse taps the corner of the mouthguard case like a superstition. I nod thanks I don't have breath for.

On my way to the bench, Chase's phone lights: NOOR. He turns the screen, gets a quick earful. "Yep… yeah, send the stills. Under-door tool marks? Copy… thank you." He pockets the phone, face gone serious. "Cameras picked up a maybe on the old scrape days," he says to me, low. "No faces, but Noor's working the pattern. She says you don't owe her a call; she'll come to you when there's something clean."

My ribs tighten, then release. Noor's card on the roster wasn't a lucky charm. It was a fuse.

After, I take Charlie to the airport lookout. We sit under the flight path on purpose. The first plane drops its shadow over us and the ground thrums up my spine like safe thunder. My pulse climbs—a rise I choose. Controlled noise. Predictable power. Chase would call it exposure. I call it remembering that not all loud things mean run.

We eat paper-tray chips and let soft-serve drip down our knuckles. The roar resets my brain like a piano chord struck clean. From here, the city is toy-small. Problems shrink long enough to breathe around them.

Across the road, we feed retired racehorses apples from our palms at Living Legends. One slobbers down Charlie's sleeve and she shrieks, laughing, shoving her hair back with the hand that wears the green ribbon. The sound unkinks something that's been coiled for months.

On the drive back I take the ring road instead of the short cut, windows down at 100, wind needling the stitches through my shirt. A tiny, manageable dare. When the speed sign flashes, I obey. It matters that I can stop.

We land on the couch sun-tired and happy, curry takeout perfuming the room, Marvel marathon doing the thinking for us.

No bills, no police statements, no guardianship forms. Just sisters. Just us.

For a few hours, I believe this could last.

In the shower that night, water roars like a distant runway and not like a siren or a fire. I close my eyes and the first thing I see is not a knife, not smoke, not green-glass eyes, but Charlie's hands wrapped right and sure, knuckles decisive.

When she's in the shower, my phone lights with the unknown number. A message: Tomorrow. Marris & Sons car park. 10. If you want.

I text before caution can form: I'll be there.

On the bench, the phone buzzes once more—Eli—then goes quiet. A smell of smoke sneaks under the window from somewhere down the block. It's only someone's dinner. It's only air. I stand there until my body believes me.

I lay out my gloves. I loop Charlie's green ribbon around my wrist and tie it off, a small promise in a room that smells like lemon and sugar and a life that is learning to be loud on purpose.

Marris & Sons

The Marris & Sons car park smells like hot bitumen and coffee. I park where I can see both exits, back to a wall, fingers counting spare keys on my ring without meaning to. A food truck hisses steam. My breath matches it—four in, six out—until my hands stop rattling.

Sam arrives without the bike, without the swagger. Black jeans. Grey tee. Eyes that used to mean wind and trouble. Now they just look tired.

We sit on the low concrete lip by the trolley bay. It's easier, being shoulder-to-shoulder with a view of escape. He talks first, getting it wrong, then right. He chews the inside of his cheek like it owes him truth, and finally says the sentence that breaks me open: "She's alive, Cas. She's been alive."

The car park tilts and rights. I grip concrete until my palms burn. "Her name?"

"Rosaleigh," he says, like a question and an apology. "She kept it. We did."

"Kept." The word knifes through the years. "Who is 'we'?"

"My aunt. Then me. It's complicated. It shouldn't have been." He swallows. "She…she knows your name."

He gives me small, ordinary details in case I need proof: mint ice cream, rabbits and double-knots, a librarian who sneaks her new-release holds, off-key singing, a stubborn left shoelace she refuses to replace because it's lucky. I look down so he can't watch those details rearrange my insides.

"Why now?" My voice is glass held together by thumb and forefinger.

"Because I finally can," he says. "And because I can't not anymore."

We set a boundary without touching—hands on knees, not each other. "Slow," he says. "Steady."

I nod like agreeing will keep the ground still.

We meet again on the old rail bridge behind the industrial estate at dusk. He shows me a photo on his phone—green ribbon on a rabbit's collar, two front teeth imperfect as courage—and I can't breathe, then I can.

"I'm not fifteen," I tell him. "I don't need you to be twenty-two."

"Seven next month," he says.

"Seven," I repeat, and the word becomes a chapel. "We'll talk again before then."

We don't touch. I walk home with the shape of her weight held like a borrowed thing.

The drive back is quiet. Every brake squeal is metal on metal. Every light is a heart monitor; I name five blue things at each intersection until the city stops sounding like a hospital. At home the music box sits where I left it—top shelf, far corner, dragonflies chipped. I wind it. The tune wobbles, and then remembers itself.

Inside: the ultrasound smudge, the soft-folded letters, the lock of hair. Only she didn't die.

"I'm sorry," I whisper to paper and song. "I didn't know."

The shower goes hot then cold—a small shock. Proof I can end a feeling when I decide to.

At Take Flight the night is loud enough to drown thought. Eli is grin-and-slur and proximity. Amelia orbits Chase like glitter with claws, bleeding poison sideways.

He corners me near the service well. "You don't know how many people want you," he says, whiskey coating his vowels. "How many see you."

"I said no." I push him back—firm, flat—until his shoulders kiss stainless. "And you ask before you touch."

He smirks. "Whatever you say, Bitesize."

The nickname lands wrong, a stone in my mouth. Over his shoulder Amelia watches, champagne straw between red lips; a small vial clinks on her bracelets like a bell for bad decisions. Later I'll see her mouth at his ear and taste the poison on his smile.

Closing is ritual: count, wipe, lock. The new deadbolt gets three checks—hand, eyes, breath—before I leave. Home is dark kitchen, music box wound twice. A third loop is too much for ribs still learning how to be houses again.

I fall asleep sideways on the couch to keep a line of sight on the door. Planes in my dreams climb and stay aloft. I wake to my own teeth unclenching.

2:11 a.m. — Voicemail from Eli.

I toe the edge of courage, swipe, and let it play.

"Hey, Cas. It's me. Uh—don't freak out. I'm fine. I'm at Unit 3, 11 Harrow Street,

Briarbank. It's not… it's not a situation, I just— Look, if you swing by later, could you bring that grey hoodie I left at yours? The one with the burn on the cuff? I think I locked myself out. Again. I'm fine. Promise. Don't tell Em. Or Chase. Okay, tell Jesse if you have to. He likes pretending he's, my dad. …You're probably asleep. Good. Okay. Okay. Bye."

The second "okay" is the kind of lie you make gentle so it doesn't spook. I text back tomorrow and put the phone face-down.

On the fridge, Detective Noor's card sags under a cheap magnet shaped like a piano key. Quiet witness. Quiet fuse.

Smoke from somebody's midnight toast threads the stairwell. For a second it's bar smoke, then car fire, then just bread. I stand

there until it's only bread.

Chapter Thirteen

Harrow Street

Unit 3, 11 Harrow Street.

Concrete forecourt. Light bleeding out of a single upstairs window like a wound. My phone is live in my hand, Noor's card under my thumb. Jesse is on speaker, voice low: "If it smells wrong, you walk."

"It already smells wrong," I whisper.

"I mean dangerous wrong."

"Everything is dangerous wrong."

The door to Unit 3 is ajar. My knuckles rap once, twice. "Eli?"

No answer. Inside smells of stale smoke, spilled sugar, chemical lemon pretending to be clean. His hoodie is on the floor where he said. A glass vial rolls lazy under my shoe and bumps the skirting.

"Eli?" I call louder.

A groan from the bathroom. The door sticks on something soft. He's slumped against the tub, eyes open but not here, lips blue at the edges.

I drop to my knees. "Hey! Eli, stay with me."

He blinks, recognition like a flicker. "Cas… I didn't— She said—" His head lolls.

I hit 000 before my brain catches up. "Unresponsive male, possible OD, Briarbank…" My voice steadies when my hands don't.

I roll him onto his side, clear his airway, count breaths. His pulse is a frantic bird. Charlie's name flashes on my screen. I hit decline and keep pressure on Eli's shoulder so he doesn't roll. "You're okay. Breathe." My voice becomes a metronome. "Breathe."

Sirens slice the night. Paramedics wedge between us, clinical and calm. Naloxone, vitals, stretcher. They ask his name; I say it like a prayer. They ask mine; I almost forget.

On the landing Amelia's silhouette shows like a cat that heard a can open. She smiles without teeth. "Such a helper," she says softly. "No wonder Chase likes you broken."

My hand curls into a fist and then unclenches. I don't swing. She glides past the paramedics — perfume like a ghost. One of the medics looks at me. "You family?"

"No." He says, "We'll call you," which means nothing.

When they're gone, I sit on the bottom stair until the night feels less like a trap. Noor's number glows on my screen. I press it.

"Detective Noor."

"It's Cas," I whisper. "He's alive but—"

"I know," she says. "I had a car close by. Stay where you are."

She arrives in plain clothes, badge on a lanyard, scarf around her hair. Not the kind of cop who makes a scene. She sits two steps below me like we're teenagers skipping class.

"You did everything right," she says quietly. "Ambulance is taking him to Western. He'll live."

"Amelia was there," I say. "She—"

"We're looking at her," Noor answers. "But you can't hold her with your bare hands. Not yet."

I nod, teeth gritted. She studies me a beat. "You've been training."

"A little."

"Good. Keep it. But don't forget: survival isn't a solo sport." She presses a card into my palm — her direct line in scrawl. "Anytime."

She stands. "Come on. I'll drive you home."

Chapter Fourteen:

Scars

Take Flight's basement smells like leather and salt and something new: trust.

Charlie sits cross-legged on the edge of the mat, head back, eyes closed, sketchbook open. Noor leans against the far wall, notepad closed, watching like she's at a play she can't stop. Chase unwraps his own hands for once. Without the gauze, his knuckles are a roadmap—scars crossing like dried rivers, a jagged welt at his shoulder disappearing under his shirt.

"You never talk about yours," I say before I think.

He glances at Charlie, then at Noor, then back at me. "War," he offers finally. "Different kind of knife."

The room hushes. He holds out a palm. "Show me yours?"

I hesitate, then peel tape from my ribs and tug my shirt up enough to show the thick X the doctor left as stitches. The room notices. My throat going dry sounds loud.

He steps closer, slow, narrating his nearness like he always does. His fingertips trace the X without pressure—only warmth. "Still the most beautiful thing I've ever seen," he says, voice rough.

My breath catches. The air between us tightens, like a held note before a kiss.

A whimper cuts through it. Charlie's nightmare breaks the moment; she jerks awake, sketchbook spilling. I drop my shirt and cross to her, pull her into me. She clings, shaking.

"It's okay," I murmur. "You're safe."

Chase gives us space. Noor closes her notepad but lingers. She watches people the way someone watches a fuse: not to tinker with it, but to know how long it will burn.

Chapter Fifteen

The Bridge

Bullying blooms in silence. Ms Patel called me in because Charlie has been walking the long way home, headphones in with no music, avoiding canteen corners where girls with glitter nails wait.

"They call me alien eyes," she says flatly at the bridge.

"They're scared of what they don't have," I say. "You're rare-pretty. We already named that."

"Rare-pretty still bleeds," she answers.

We go to the old rail bridge—Sam and I used to haunt it. We lean on the rusted rail, and she sketches the skyline upside down. I tell her about falling down, getting up, not waiting for permission to take space.

"I'm not letting them shrink you," I promise.

"You're barely keeping yourself big," she shoots back.

"Fair," I admit. "So we'll learn together."

We run mitt drills until her laugh cuts the dusk, sharp and alive. A train passes underneath and the bolts applaud. Later Sam texts: *Rosie wants to see you. Just us. Park?*

I stare at the message. Above the bridge planes cut the sky into lanes of light. Below, Noor's unmarked car waits like a quiet chord.

16

- Subject expanding protective circle to include sister; showing incremental exposure to former trauma sites.

- Sam re-entered picture with minor. Monitor for custodial and safety issues.

- Amelia/Eli link strengthening. Next action: approach Amelia under pretext of licensing check.

— S. Noor

Chapter Sixteen:

Into the

Unknown

The mat smells like rubber and old sweat. I lie flat, breath sawing, ceiling lights blurring into watery halos. Chase is next to me, one arm shielding his eyes, the other still holding my hand where our palms found each other after a clean cross clipped his jaw.

"Nice form," he says, light back in his voice now that the adrenaline has exhausted itself into ache.

I turn my head. His mouth blooms pink on one side. "Worth it," he says when I try to apologize.

The quiet seats itself between us like something patient. It's the kind of silence that isn't empty—it's waiting. I think if I don't say it now, I might never. The words come out ragged.

"A child I thought died," I say to the rafters, "is alive."

He doesn't move. Pipes tick. Cupid's Wing hums a single chord through the floorboards, oblivious to the fact everything is about to change.

"She's mine," I say. The last word snaps. "She's been alive this whole time."

My fingers fizz on the mat. I breathe in four, out six until electricity loosens into ache. He doesn't tell me to breathe. He doesn't tell me it's okay. He threads his fingers through mine and stays, anchoring us to the canvas until my lungs recalibrate on their own.

A throat clears on the stairs. We both sit up.

Emily, Jesse, Eli file in like a badly rehearsed chorus. Behind them, heels and perfume: Amelia. She glides in, impossible in a way that says the room belongs to eyes, not to people.

Emily's face is already soft. "What happened?" she asks.

Amelia's gaze finds our linked hands. "Whatever this is," she purrs, "you'll both regret it."

"Time," Jesse says. Not a threat. A boundary.

Eli looks off-balance—under-slept, over-poured. Amelia's arm brushes him; a crystal chime. My stomach drops at the pattern I don't want to see.

I don't argue. I touch down with my feet and make the street before I can be interrogated. I sit on the curb with my back to brick, knees hugged, trying to fold myself into a smaller shape. Sirens unhook a memory; for a beat I'm under hospital fluorescents again. I list five things—brick, gum, poster, bolt, sky—until the present sits down beside me like a steady friend.

Home is a rummage—music box wound too long, song scraping to a stop. I run cold water on my face until the sting blinks. I say it into the empty kitchen because saying it helps make it true: "There's a girl. She's… mine."

I picture a green ribbon and a rabbit that sits for clumsy hands. I breathe the thought into being until it doesn't cut like glass.

Time is an orbit. I find my feet at the same curb outside Take Flight more than once in the week that follows. I am no longer the person who toes an edge and dares the fall; I am the person who wants the edge and chooses the step behind it. For now, that is

enough.

Interlude — Eli, 2:11 A.M. Voicemail That Exists Whether You Listen Or Not

Door won't shut right. Or it shuts and locks me out of my head. Same thing. Apartment smells like old carpet and citrus cleaner. Amelia left a smile on my glass and something in my pocket. "It's nothing," she said; "edge stuff. Fun." I don't like the word *fun* when it tastes like attic dust.

I'm calling because you keep not dying and I want the recipe. Joke. Kinda.

Harrow Street. Unit 3. Hoodie—the one with the burn on the cuff from a candle at Emily's. Don't tell Em. Or Chase. Tell Jesse if you have to. He likes pretending he's my dad.

Okay. Okay. Bye.

The message hangs on the phone like a sound that isn't ready to leave.

Interlude — Detective Noor: Case Notes

- **Location:** Take Flight (rear door); **Action:** New deadbolt installed; prior tool marks consistent with under-door rake (homemade). Timing of previous rattles aligns with two other late-night low-grade attempts in four-block radius. Pattern: patient.

- **Victim:** Cassianna S. — consistent statements, avoids dramatization, underreports pain. High risk for traumatization. Protective factor: younger sister, Charlie (15).

- **Staff / Associates:** Amelia B. — non-employee but frequent, proximity to staff (noted leaning/support of Eli), introduces alcohol/vials; influence vector. Eli [staff] shows signs of substance misuse and risky proximity.

- **Leads:** Voicemail trace leads to Unit 3, Harrow St (Briarbank). Cross-reference with noise complaints (glass break, shouting) last month — possible escalation pattern.

- **Plan:** Quiet welfare follow-up on Unit 3; canvass Harrow & Denby for CCTV; check tenancy roster; avoid spooking victim; arrange gentle touchpoint with Cas when appropriate. Continue to monitor Amelia/Eli links.

— S. Noor

Glass Rabbit

The hospital waiting room smelled like warmed plastic and burnt toast, the kind of smell that pretends it's food so your stomach will believe you're allowed to be human. Eli sat hunched as if gravity had learned new tricks on him. Hoodie up, hands worrying the frayed cuff where fire had nicked the fabric months ago—little self-harm souvenirs Amelia called "edge stuff." He looked too small for the chair, sleeves two inches too long, shadowed eyes that didn't match his clothes.

"Hey," I said the word like a rope. He blinked and tried a smile that folded at the edges. It did not reach his eyes.

"Cas," he said. His voice was thin and surprised, like someone who'd been handed a thing he hadn't earned. "You—don't come in. You left a crate in the alley last time and—"

"You left me a voicemail at two AM," I cut. "You said you were fine twice, so I thought—"

He looked at his hands. "Yeah. 'I'm fine' is… it's a spell." He laughed once and it sounded like someone scraping branches. "Doesn't work."

A nurse called his name and he rose like he'd been pulled by thread. He moved as if his limbs were borrowed. I watched him go and my chest tightened in a familiar, animal way. I'd pulled him from the tub three nights before, palms full of panic and emergency room lights. He'd lived. He'd come back to a world that still expected him to be useful, and he was doing his best to fold into usefulness like someone trying to fit into another person's jacket.

Sam found me in the corridor. He had an envelope in his hands so thick it bent at the middle. We'd met in Marris & Sons the week I'd found out a daughter I thought gone was alive; Sam smelled like petrol and something softer—mint gum, maybe, or the faint ash of nerves.

"I—" He held up the envelope. "They ran more tests after Rosie's last admission. The clinic called. It's… they've flagged hereditary markers. They say she might need a transplant."

Words rearranged themselves into new shapes. "Transplant?" I repeated, like testing them in my mouth to see if they were real vocab.

"Bone marrow. They want to test close family." He watched me as if the next breath was a cliff. "They asked for contact numbers. I… I didn't know how to tell you."

My knees remembered the same small shock they'd learned at the underpass. The world narrowed to the edge of a sink and an X-stitch where the seatbelt had been. "Where is she?" I asked instead, because doing the factual things kept panic from congealing into terror.

"Out near my aunt's. She's… Rosie calls the rabbit 'Sir Wiggles.' She likes mint ice cream. She ties her shoelace to keep it lucky." His voice softened, too small for the things it carried. "They said family testing first. They wanted me to get you before it was a list."

Something hot slid under my ribs and lodged there where grief and hope had once argued. "When?"

"Soon," Sam said. "They want samples. They said if there's a match—"

"No," I said, and the word was a brick. It landed and then built a wall: *I will be there.*

The rest of the day unraveled in small, sharp motions. Phone calls; a nurse reading out forms like they were recipes—one measure of consent, two of disclaimers. Noor texted one-line pragmatism and a folded kindness: *Good. Quiet welfare on Harrow done. Call before you go so we don't overlap.**

Eli's number pinged with a short message: *Sorry. Thanks. Dont tell Em I cried in the bathroom.* I read it twice and felt both anger and an odd, tender pity. I'd pulled him out of a bath that smelled of lemon and bleach while someone with perfume like a weapon watched from the landing. He had a new bruise at his temple and the faraway look of a person who'd met a doorway they thought they might walk through.

That night sleep refused me. It staged a slow mutiny—eyes open and muscles stone. Sleep paralysis hit like an invisible hand pressing my chest into the mattress; my jaw felt bolted, my breath a bird trapped in a jar. For nearly a minute I knew everything down to the pattern of the plaster. I felt the heavy, knowing presence of a dark thing at the foot of the bed and the whole catalogue of past nights whispered their coordinates to me: siren, metal, a green glare of headlights. Then my limbs stuttered back to life and I screamed soundless into the pillow, raw as if I'd burned my tongue.

Charlie woke before I could pull my breath back together. She sat up, hair an explosion, eyes huge and red-rimmed. One look at me and she did not ask the adult questions kids sometimes ask. She simply said, "Cas?" like a small tool, ready.

"I'm here," I croaked. The mantra tasted of hospital soap.

She slid off the mattress and came to the kitchen like a little house. She smelled like the day—ink and strawberries—and reached for my wrists the way only children do: with an exactness that bypasses shame. "You were screaming."

"I was," I admitted. My hands were knotted with the tape from training—red wraps that felt like armor and also like confession. "I'm… tired."

She pressed both of her palms to my cheek like she was trying to make me a map of what was real. "We've got art club tomorrow," she said. "Ms Patel says I should bring the shards."

"I'll come," I said, the promise a small, functional thing.

Half an hour later the panic came again—rapid now, a scattered, flapping animal. My fingers tremored until the tea slid and made a small, wet apology on the benchtop. My heart galloped raw. The kitchen was too small and my chest too loud; the hallway light a serrated thing. I tried to breathe by the numbers and the numbers fled.

I called Noor because she was the unalarming adult we had. "Feeling naked," I said, useless and white-lipped. "Can you—someone—be around?"

Her voice on the phone was even. "Chase and Emily can come. I'll coordinate quietly. You don't have to explain."

Before I could hang up, there was a knock and then two sets of boots and a warm, boss-voice: "Cas? Window checks done. We're here."

They sat like a cord on the couch. Emily's presence was practical: a cup of water, constellations of advice in two sentences. Chase was quieter—slower in his movements as if he measured how to be big without swallowing a smaller person. He asked only what I needed: "Do you want noise? Silence? Do you want me to talk you through breath counts?"

I hated needing it. I hated how small it made me and how much relief there was when someone answered anyway. I picked silence. He cued a metronome with his voice. *In four. Out six.* The syllables threaded my lungs into rhythm and the panic spent itself into a bruise.

At one point Charlie came out with her sketchbook and climbed onto my lap. She smelled like graphite and the green ribbon she'd tied to her wrist. She traced the crease where my ribs still itched and whispered, "It's okay. I'm here. We will do the testing."

That last sentence steadied me more than anything Chase's hands could do.

When dawn knifed the kitchen window I called the clinic. They booked me for the swab and blood draw: initial screens, HLA typing. Sam texted me the appointment link for the next day. Noor's note arrived: *Quiet check will be on route. Don't decide on anything massive without sleep. But—you said you wanted to, so we're ready when you are.*

I stood in the doorway and wound the music box until the dragonfly's wings clicked. For a long while I sat with the noise until my fingers loosened and my chest no longer felt like it belonged to someone else.

Eli sent one short message that morning: *Thanks. For before. Don't tell Em I said it, but I… I owe you.* I typed four words and deleted them twice before settling on: *You're not alone.*

When I left the apartment to go for the test, Charlie tugged my sleeve. "Bring a picture," she said, fierce and practical, "in case you forget who you're doing it for."

I smiled and ironed the ribbon into my wrist like a contract. One small thing, one very loud decision: *I will be here.*

The clinic smelled like coffee and paper forms. I sat in the chair and rolled up my sleeve. When the nurse took the sample, I thought of a tiny rabbit collar with a green ribbon and of a child who liked mint ice cream and stubborn shoelaces. I thought of Eli's fragile smile and of Noor's calm voice. I thought of Charlie's hand on my palm and chose breath, again and again, until the fear, for now, was a thing we could measure.

When the nurse taped my arm, she said the procedural things—how long the tests would take, where results would come—but I only heard the part that mattered: they will test. If there's a match, they'll call.

Outside, the sky was grey with the kind of rain that promises to be steady, not heroic. I tucked the test confirmation into my wallet like a bandage and walked back to the tram with my head high enough to see the city move under its small, ordinary rules.

There were things I could not control—Eli's bad nights, Amelia's lit smiles, the way old things remembered their scripts—but there were things I could try to change. I had a name now. I had a file being built across hospital and precinct lines. I had the creak of people who would not let me fall unmoored: a detective who left her card like a fuse, a boss who would cross a barroom for me, a sister with a ribbon.

And beneath all of it, this: a tiny girl whose life might tilt toward a future because I chose to stand in a room and bleed into a tube. It felt like the smallest, most monstrous kind of bravery—and also, maybe, the kind that keeps you breathing.

Charlie's POV — Rare-Pretty

The bus window is a watercolor: my face smeared twice—blue and brown. I tie the green ribbon Cas left on the bench around my wrist, knot inside so it presses when my fingers close. Signal and armour. If anyone asks why green, I'll say grass grows through concrete. Rabbits wear collars. It looks good making trouble.

At school Nadia and Liv orbit like parentheses. "Contacts?" Nadia offers. "A condition?" Liv supplies. I press the ribbon with a thumb. "Heterochromia," I say. "Means I can see twice as many bad choices." It shuts them up. Taylor shows up brave as a pocketknife. She notices my ribbon and tacks another piece to her shoelace like a flag.

Ms. Patel says, "Bring that line to art club." I tuck the instruction in my pocket like a ticket. The art room smells like charcoal and promise. I draw shards until they become wings at a step back. The magpie outside the window watches me like a critic.

I text Detective Noor with the voicemail detail because adults make a better net than we do. Her reply is kind in a way that feels like sunlight on knees. *If anyone gives you grief for being rare-pretty, tell them Detective Noor says it's a superpower.* I laugh then. My whole chest does that messy proud thing around people who make the world behave.

At home Cas smells like the safe part of the city tonight. She squeezes my shoulder like a door checks its latch. "Good?" she asks.

"Getting there," I say, and show her the ribbon like it's a passport.

When she goes to bed the number that was unknown before pings on the screen. *Tomorrow. Marris & Sons car park. 10. If you want.* She texts: I'll be there. I knot the ribbon to my backpack strap like I can anchor her with sight.

If the world is loud, I'll learn to be louder.

Interlude — Detective Noor: Case Notes

- **Incoming:** Charlie S. (minor) texts re: Unit 3 / Eli voicemail. Content: minimization patterns flagged. Good outreach.

- **Action:** Quiet welfare check queued; camera canvass Harrow & Denby underway. Liaison with school for low-key support (art teacher flagged as ally). Avoid alarming Cas. Continue monitoring Amelia/Eli association and tenancy roster for Unit 3.

- **Note:** Child coping ritual (green ribbon) indicates resourcefulness. Consider school liaison contact for bullying mitigation. Maintain contact channel open via Cas.

— S. Noor

Chapter Seventeen:

Blood Ties

Hospital antiseptic is the sound of things pretending to be tidy. I sit on a vinyl chair with a bandage over my forearm, Sam across from me like a man who's been asked to remember the shape of a promise. Charlie is slumped next to Emily, ribbon blinking like a little emergency light.

The doctor's mouth makes small, careful shapes. "You're a match," he says.

Relief thuds into my ribs and then something else unravels—fear arranging itself into every "and" that follows. "And?" I ask.

"Given her presentation, we recommend bone-marrow harvest from you. Lower chronic GVHD risk than peripheral collection. There are risks." He slides the consent forms across like breathing things: bleeding, infection, nerve pain, anaesthetic. I sign anyway. Hope is honest even when its language is ugly.

Sam breathes like he's standing under scaffolding and refusing to let it fall. Chase reads the forms without comment. Emily rubs circles across Charlie's back as if she can trace a map toward safety.

Later, Sam sits in my room without crowding. "If she makes it," he says, like he's distributing credit, "it's because of you."

"We both did this," I say. The sentence feels like a rope.

"We were kids," he says. "We were scared."

"We were scared," I repeat, because scared is the only true word that doesn't try to make the past smaller.

A knock. Amelia's perfume arrives like daylight in a glass bottle. She steps into the doorway with a paper cup in hand—charity tea and thinly disguised spectacle. "Tragic," she intones, and sets the cup with the casual cruelty of someone practicing a sport.

Chase is on his feet before I can find a voice. "Not a good time," he says, and he is a wall the rest of us get to lean on.

She leaves a lipstick print on the rim of the cup—territory, signature. When she's gone Chase sets a vending-machine tea down and lets out a breath the room seems to hold for him.

Pre-op is practical, clinical: remove jewellery, change here, breathe there. A nurse with kindness in her eyes asks the question that lives over everything: "Will it be enough?"

"For her—yes," I say. "For you—rest." Her answer is honest. The rest is for later.

They wheel me under lights that do their best to be kind. I count backwards because it is the only arithmetic that steadies me: ninety-four, ninety-three, the world narrowing to the inside of a skull and the sound of someone's footsteps at the window like a clock.

When I wake, the ceiling is bright and chirpy and not the siren that used to own me. Charlie sits studiously in a chair with her ribbon looped like a crown. Sam stands by the window, a shape keeping watch. Chase's hand finds mine, steady and unshy. "You did the hard part," he says.

We spend the first days in that tender, weirdly normal space hospitals allow: paperwork signed with shaky ink, visitors arriving with terrible food and better intention, Noor's voice a low constant across the line—checking, offering, describing patterns without dumping them in our laps. She doesn't promise anything she can't keep.

Outside, Amelia's orbit tightens at the bar. Eli drifts somewhere between penitent and fraying. Jesse is a door wearing a human face. Emily steers like a lighthouse with a beer glass for ballast.

In quieter moments I stare at Rosie's photo on my phone and wonder how a life can be both claim and gift. Sam apologises in small, unnecessary ways until I tell him the one honest thing I can: "She deserves a chance."

He nods, like we both thought that would be the easy part.

The day after surgery Sam brings Rosaleigh for a short, sunburst visit. She is small and fierce and everything ordinary about children; she pulls a loose thread from the blanket and ties it into a knot like she's casting a spell. My chest folds and unravels with the weight of her breath.

Chase watches her, and there's the thing—an almost-ask that is not yet a question—on the edge of his face. I don't know what to do with the way my heart wants to open and then stay closed. I rest my hand on his; he squeezes without taking more than I give.

Amelia stands a distance away, measuring. Jordan, her friend, bobs like an observer who remembers only the fun parts. The pattern Noor has flagged keeps knitting itself: influence, proximity, small cruelties packaged as confidence.

Noor arrives in the corridor the way sunlight arrives—plain shoes, plain voice. She doesn't make a scene. "We're building a file," she says quietly later. "We'll close loops. I need time." She speaks into the space between us like she's knitting a rope. That's all I want for now.

Time is the currency of the small things: a cheesecake that tastes like triumph, a borrowed show that makes us laugh, Charlie drawing a halo around Rosie on a paper napkin. I keep that napkin in my pocket, a talisman.

Night pulls the curtain and I check my phone like a litmus strip. Noor texts: Unit 3 welfare check done. Eli responsive. Will coordinate follow-up with ambulance team. Amelia under observation for behavioural pattern. We'll talk soon.

I place the phone face down and feel something settle—not a cage, but a room with doors I can test.

Chapter Eighteen:

Waiting for Answers

The wrong beep wakes me—foreign and sharp. The anaesthetic leaves light like knives. My body remembers other alarms.

"MET call, Ward Twelve, Bed Seven," the PA cracks in a distant voice. Not us. My chest ignores the difference. Panic has a clean edge. I jerk; pain snaps bright along my hips and spine where bone gave what it could.

"Cas—hey." A nurse's hand is calm on my shoulder, another steady on the rail. "That call isn't for you. Breathe with me."

Chase fills the doorway like he belongs in the frame. "With me, Bitesize," he says, low. "In four. Out six."

I find the old seatbelt arc at my collarbone and count. In one, two, three, four. Out two, three, four, five, six. The floor steadies. The edges put their teeth away.

Emily stands at the foot of the bed, blinking back tears. Sam hangs back with new rules for his hands. Jesse checks the corridor the way soldiers check horizons and leaves the door as a door.

They bring a pole with lemon-bright bags and hang them like offerings. "Product looks good," the transplant coordinator says, voice softer than this building is allowed to be. "We'll courier to her unit the minute the final checks are done."

"I need the bathroom," I say, because dignity is a kind of analgesic.

The nurse clips my line and walks me the five slow steps. "I'll be right outside," she says, meaning doors and time.

Under the fluorescent mirror my body is a place I don't recognise: harvest dressings butterflying my hips, bruises blooming midnight-dark. The knife scars from the bar have stitched into a hard X—shiny, pale—marking the place someone chose and I didn't. PTSD isn't a pamphlet; it's the way skin starts to look borrowed and wrong and shame knocks on the door when you breathe.

"Cas?" Chase's voice, patient at the threshold. "Company or quiet?"

"Quiet," I say, because it's both lie and truth.

I touch the X with two fingers: a landmark. I name five square things—tile, tile, tile, tile, paper dispenser—and say my name inside my head until it sounds like mine again.

"I'm here," I tell the girl in the glass. "You are mine."

When I open the door Chase is at the window, hands in pockets, not posing as a promise. Emily nudges me with feral softness: a touch and then space, like someone who knows how to hold.

Back in bed the day remembers its shape. "Engraftment is a process," the doctor says. "Days to weeks. Expect fevers. Expect scares. Use your call bell before getting up."

"No promises," I say. "I'll try."

A text buzzes Charlie's phone on the chair arm; she startles but shows me without being asked. The message is small but bright: Mr Rowan (art therapy) — I'm on the children's floor Wednesdays/Fridays. If you ever want a room with paper, not questions, I keep both. You can just sit. Or draw. Or not.

Ms. Patel says you have a line worth protecting.

"Do it," I tell Charlie, trying to make it a doorway not a duty.

Detective Noor's reply slides in beneath it: Update received. Proud of you. Tell the loud things I said to take a number.

Charlie pockets her phone and leaves with the peculiar stomp-and-float that only fifteen-year-olds own.

Quiet comes back in new forms. Sam sits by the window, pretending the sky will answer. Jesse brings allegedly-not-hateful tea. Emily bullies me into two more sips and a corner of biscuit.

Chase doesn't sit. He leans his shoulder on the doorframe and holds a perimeter until someone else can.

"Teach me a drill," I say, because waiting chews.

He breathes: "Eyes closed. See the bag. Hands up. Jab—breathe on impact. Cross— breathe. Slip left. Slip right. Frame. Knee up the middle if they crowd you."

I do it lying down—ridiculous and holy. The punching bag in my head becomes a pole with two lemon-bright blessings. Jab. Cross. Slip. Frame. Knee. Breathe.

When I open my eyes, he looks at me like I didn't just move air. "It counts," he says, catching an apology undecided on my tongue, and pockets it.

Evening bruises the window. Somewhere a kid laughs in another ward; a pump apologises elsewhere. The coordinator pops in with the small word I hear as a miracle:

"Viable." She keeps talking but I only hear that.

"They've started," Chase says, folding forward like a man braced for good news. "It's a waiting game."

Relief hits so hard I shut my eyes until the world softens. "Okay," I breathe. "Okay."

Charlie returns at dusk with pastel-smudged fingers and the kind of quiet that's better than noise. She climbs into the bed beside me and arranges herself like we're two pieces that still fit. "You came back," she says.

"Every time," I answer.

"For me," she insists.

"For you," I say. "For her."

Night shrinks footsteps and opens space. Emily nestles the spare blanket over my legs.

Sam sits outside Rosaleigh's door like a guardian. Jesse texts a photo of Charlie burrito-wrapped on someone's couch as proof the world contains jokes.

At some point my hand drifts toward the space between us. Chase finds it and folds our fingers together like something he's allowed to know how to do in the dark.

I stand up to walk the corridor once, a slow loop to check windows and count tiles. The children's art room is lit and warm; through the narrow rectangular viewing pane in the door I see Charlie sitting at a low table, hands busy with paper.

And him—Mr Rowan—sitting a few feet away, patient, a soft pencil in his hand. He's the grown-up everyone trusts: calm voice, measured smile. He nudges a pastel toward

Charlie, and she reaches for it without a flicker of fear.

I linger because I need to look. The glass is double, slightly reflective. Rowan turns and his eyes find the door—then find me through the reflection. For a heartbeat everything rearranges: his gaze slips into mine and it's the same shape as the intruder's eyes from the night that split me open. Calm green, a small lightning nick at the brow—an old, precise detail that lifts the same old panic like dust. My stomach drops out. Recognition is a hard, hot thing.

I don't move. I swallow slow and pull the sleeve over my hand to hide the tremor. Charlie laughs at something he says—an unassuming sound—and Rowan's mouth curves, professional, careful. He doesn't stand. He doesn't follow my line of sight. But for a moment I hold that look—his eyes on mine—and a cold that isn't the hospital fills me.

I step back without making a sound and find Emily's hand on my shoulder before I know I need it. "You good?" she asks, soft like an anchor.

"No," I say. The one word is small and true. I don't tell her what the eyes mean—not yet. There are things you have to see yourself before you give them names. I let the moment file itself under watch.

Back in the room I close the curtain in tiny folds and move like someone making a plan nobody will notice. I don't tell Charlie. I don't make a scene. I breathe in four, out six until the rawness softens to manageable.

Waiting isn't nothing. It's a series of small fights you do lying down and an inventory of choices you make while the world hums on. Tonight one of those choices is to watch, to catalogue, to hold the recognition for later.

I'm getting better at waiting—and at the kind of quiet that keeps the people I love small and out of sight of certain eyes.

Charlie's POV — Paper Shields

Hospitals try to smell like lemons and end up smelling like worry with homework. The children's floor is louder than Cas's ward— TV laughs, an IV wheel that squeaks, a toddler who hasn't learned mercy. A sign says ART THERAPY with letters that look exhausted and kind. I follow the arrows because I am good at following arrows when nobody hands me a map.

The art room is a miracle of paper. Stacks and stacks—thick, thin, glossy, rough—like someone decided trees get second lives. The trolley holds pastels in a rainbow that deserves the name. There's a window that looks over the car park and makes the sky feel closer.

"Charlie?" he says, like we were picking up a conversation.

"Ms Patel told on me," I try for a joke. It lands as a small thing.

"She bragged," the art-therapist says, professional smile. "Paper, not questions?"

I sit. He hands me a soft pencil. "House rule: it doesn't have to be good. It has to be true."

I draw glass first—shards of triangle, a sliver like a comet—and thread a thin green ribbon through them, vein-line, river-line. Piano keys grow along the edge of the page because sound is a stair you can climb without leaving the chair. Two boxing gloves hang from a nail I draw in the corner; they're too big and I leave them that way on purpose.

Smoke curls along the bottom, a quiet animal that knows how to slip under doors.

He doesn't hover. He refills the crayons like a bartender. He laughs in the good way. "Anything you want to say out loud?" he asks as if the room could be both a studio and a safe place.

"Only that I hate waiting," I tell him.

"That's a thesis," he says. "How does waiting look?"

I shade a rectangle darker and darker until the paper complains. I stop before it tears because I am kinder to paper than I sometimes am to myself.

My phone buzzes: a group chat that's mean and stupid.

Ur eyes are so extra

attention is free babe

do they let you keep contacts in for surgery lol

I tape the screen facedown. New technique: Shut Up, Phone.

He smiles, approved. He slides a sticky note across with a little breathing reminder: four in / six out. Name five squares. "When those louds get loud," he says, tapping the note. "Boss them around." I pocket it.

Back in the lift the doors open and Amelia steps out with perfume like a knife. She talks into a phone like a stage director of cruelty: "Tragic brings foot traffic," she says and laughs. I stand still until she moves past.

At the vending machine Noor is muttering at almonds like she's got a side job rescuing vending machines. She spots me.

"Almonds or chips?" she asks, as if the world needed another choice.

"Chips are louder," I say.

"Noor notes things," she says, like it's a brag. "Mr Rowan texted—if you need a room with paper and no questions, you've got one. If anyone gives you grief tell me and I'll let the almonds handle it."

"You're supposed to be a detective," I say. "Not a snack enforcer."

"Delegation is leadership," she answers, and her mouth twitches.

When I get back to Cas's room she's sideways in the bed like a guard, Chase a bracket at the window, Emily halfway through a negotiation with the nurse about contraband coffee, Jesse pretending a hand-hygiene brochure is a thriller. I tape my drawing to the foot of her bed like a small shield.

"That ribbon," Chase says when he looks.

"Green," I tell him, daring him to be sentimental.

"Good choice," he says without explaining, and his not-explaining feels better than adults who over-explain oxygen.

Later I practice the stance Jesse taught me—feet under shoulders, knees soft, chin down, invisible gloves up. I am fifteen and also stout.

A group chat pings in with the usual noise; I don't feed it. I text Taylor instead: airport later when life isn't a building? chips are louder. She replies ok. bring ribbon. I smile. Tiny. Teethed.

On a detour back to the children's floor there's a door with a paper star labelled ROSA. The window is a small rectangle, and I see a small hand tap the rail twice like telling time. A nurse moves into view and blocks it. I touch the glass with two fingers the way people touch maps: small and precise.

I stick my drawing to the corridor wall beside the star. Under it I write on a sticky note: for R. — from C. (wings are for staying, too)

When I return to my chair I count five squares—tile, tile, exit sign, noticeboard, the window in Mum's door—four in, six out. The loud things queue respectfully.

Later, Casper sleeps with the arm that watches the door. I tuck my green ribbon into my pocket so I won't play with it until it breaks.

I am the girl with a glass wing, a crooked bow, and a stance. I am not smaller than the room says I am.

Also, I want chips.

• Unit 3 welfare check completed. Eli responsive; ambulance follow-up arranged. No immediate criminality established on site; witness statements pending.

• Take Flight: Amelia B. — non-employee frequent; pattern of proximity and drink-delivery to staff (Eli). Influence vector: social access + alcohol; monitor.

• New name surfaced via volunteer list: Thomas (T.) Rowan — registered as art therapist via regional placements. Background checks: clean public record; references from closed (institutional) programs; reported history: fiancé deceased in road crash linked to same collision that killed Cassianna & partner's parents (documents matched by hospital records). **FLAG**: approach Rowan with caution; do not spook family/victim (Cas) — maintain soft contact.

• Next steps: canvass volunteer references, request hospital CCTV short clips (clinic wing -> children's art room windows), quiet welfare follow-ups for Unit 3 and nearby tenancies. Maintain contact with Cas via scheduled check-ins. — S. Noor

Chapter Nineteen:

Cracks in the Glass

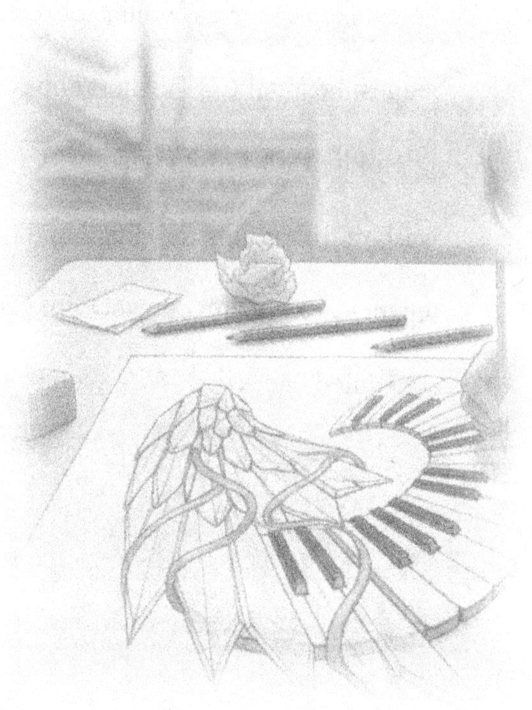

Not everyone believes this is the right thing.

Jesse corners me outside the hospital cafeteria, voice low and honed. He looks like a man who learned to carry steadiness in his jaw. "You're about to risk your life for a kid you didn't know existed a week ago. What happens to Charlie if something goes wrong?"

His question cuts in the place I already live with: late nights counting respirator beeps, calendar pages marked with forms, the arithmetic of survival that never balances. "She's my daughter," I say. The sentence sits heavy and exact. "I won't abandon her."

"And if you die?" His eyes flick past my shoulder to where Charlie sits at a sticky table head-down on her phone, fingers angry. "She loses you. Both of them lose you. Think about that."

There's no answer that fits that question and still lets me breathe. Doing nothing and watching Rosaleigh slip where my marrow might have held—it feels worse than a thousand deaths. I put my hands flat against cold stairwell tile and count—four in, six out—until the urge to run eases into something I can carry.

Later, Emily finds me by the lifts as if she always knows where I'll try to hide. She presses a paper cup into my fingers like medicine. "He's scared," she says, and her voice has pity in it but no condemnation. She's beautiful in a messy, human way and I want to tell her she doesn't owe us fear, but the words dissolve. "We all are. Don't let him set the math. This isn't choosing between them. It's saving a child who deserves a chance."

That should be answer enough. It doesn't make the cracks stop appearing, only sharper. Charlie's silence is a chasm between us. Jesse's doubt maps onto my ribs. Eli's unease—slippery, tired—follows him in uneasy circles around ward doors. Amelia's orbit feels like a bruise at the edges of everything. Each step toward transplant feels like walking across glass; each breath nicking something I thought callused.

I take two flights of stairs, two down, not to run but to prove to myself my legs still listen. At the top landing I press my thumb to the seatbelt arc above my collarbone and count until the twitch in my fingers eases.

Alarms beep three floors away and a calm wordless calculation holds me: name five blue things on the fire poster, watch the numbers in my head rearrange themselves into safety.

On the children's floor, Ms Patel gives a small nod and a paper cup for Charlie—her way of saying the place belongs to the patient for the moment. I pausing by the art room and catch the edge of my sister's new drawing in the doorway: piano keys kissing the edge of a glass wing, a thin green ribbon threaded through the shards. She doesn't look up; she is all concentration and the secret, private life of a fifteen-year-old being brave.

Night, at home, smells like lemon soap and overused hospital corridors. I stand at the window and let an ambulance rattle the pane. The instruction that's been my whisper for years—run—flares and I tell it stay. I practice small dares: leave the flat for an hour, come back; turn off the light in the hall and listen; put the key in the lock and choose to enter. Little choices, like thread through a seam.

Charlie won't meet my eyes when I say goodnight; she shoves a hand through her hair and chooses words like armour. Still she won't sleep without my door cracked. We hover in that threshold, two reflections that can't quite match.

"Text me if you wake," I say.

"Obviously," she answers, which in Charlie's language means a promise already kept.

When the building breathes, I lie sideways on the sheets where I can see the door. I count with the machines down the hall until tide replaces terror. Glass holds. For now.

Before I turn in, I fish in Emily's apron pocket for a wipe and my fingers brush something that wasn't there yesterday: a narrow instruction leaflet the size of a pill packet, folded small. A name I don't expect stares at me for a second—positive, then not—and for a beat the world reorders. Emily catches me with her eyes and gives me a look that reads confession and fear.

"Not telling yet," she mouths, and the slow, ridiculous grin she gives is a terrible, beautiful thing. Another life is already rearranging; another risk is folding into our small orbit. I put the leaflet back and choose not to ask. Some things are private until they're not.

Outside school the next day, Charlie tells me, quiet, "He helped in the canteen today. Told me I had good hands for drawing. Gave me a pastel." Her voice is small with delight. "He… he gets it."

Something in my stomach eases and then flips. Relief — and a prickle of wrong I can't name. I tuck my hand into my pocket like I'm checking for a missing piece and find instead the feeling of eyes that don't belong. For now, it's only a shadow I can check in mirrors.

I go to bed with the seatbelt arc pressed under my palm and a list of questions I'll never ask aloud. The world is more breakable and more precious than the math suggests. I sleep anyway—brief, tentative, clinging to the small, stubborn proof of breaths gone right.

Chapter Twenty:

The Procedure

The day arrives with all the procedural calm of something big that refuses to be ordinary.

Pre-op is instruction in white. Remove jewellery. Sign here. Breathe there. Bone marrow harvest under general anaesthetic: needles into the backs of my hips, hours of rest afterward, a dull, burning wake-up for a little girl named Rosaleigh who has already stolen so much of my future I can't imagine losing her again.

Sam is there; sleeves rolled like a man who's learned to stand in the place he used to flee. He doesn't reach to touch me—touch feels too loud—but his eyes say enough: fear braided with gratefulness and an ember of the man who used to make the world feel like a place with edges to climb rather than cliffs to fall from.

Chase is on the other side, sleeves up, the kind of safe you can lean a broken thing against. He gives my hand a quiet squeeze— anchor and apology and promise in one press.

Between them I find the balance I learned the long way. I want to be reckless; I want to be sensible. The day makes those two choices press together until I can't tell which is louder.

Charlie bursts into the pre-op room at the last possible minute, Emily a sweating shadow at her heels. My sister's face is streaked with tears and defiance; she throws herself at me like she's trying to stop the world from taking me away. "Don't die," she whispers into my hair, fierce and childish and perfectly honest. "Don't you dare."

I smooth her hair and shape the word "I won't" into a promise even if my mouth still trembles. "Promise," I say, because sometimes saying the thing aloud makes the universe line up.

They wheel me through long fluorescent corridors that smell like lemon and bleach pretending to be clean. The anaesthetic staff smile the friendly, professional smiles people use when they can't make miracles but can make you comfortable enough to go toward them. I think fast thoughts—rabbit collars, mint ice cream, Rosie's crooked laugh—and count my way backward until the numbers tug me under.

Sam stands helpless at the rail; Chase's grip on the corridor handle blanches white. Emily presses lips into her phone like prayer. Jesse is there, took up post at the end of the hall like a man who will not be moved. The anaesthetist asks if I'm ready. "No," I say, the truth like a small knife. "Yes," I add.

The room folds and does its work. Ninety-nine. Ninety-eight. I hold Charlie's face in memory. I hold Sam's quiet apology. I hold Chase's steadying hand. The last thing I see is the stubborn, brave curl of my sister's upper lip, the promise in her eyes.

The procedure is less violent than the memory of the underpass, more clinical, less cinematic—but it takes things. The recovery tastes like lemon and dull metal. My hips ache in a way that says victory and theft in the same sentence.

When I wake, there's a small, enormous force around me: machines, the polite chatter of nurses, the looped beep of life. The nurse tucks a pillow under my knees and calls the transplant coordinator, who tells me, softly and businesslike, that the product was couriered and is on the way. Engraftment, she explains, is waiting. There will be fevers, there will be good days and days that will feel like betrayals. She offers the sort of empathy that understands the map but not the map's edges.

Later, in the quiet of the ward, Sam brings a small, sticky hand into the room. Rosaleigh is fierce as a miniature monarch, grinning with the single-minded certainty of childhood. She tugs at the blanket and tells us about a librarian who hides new books for her. She makes a game of tying the knot in my scarf the wrong way on purpose. When she leans into me to be held, the world shrinks to the size of her ribcage and the truth moves from a rumor to a fact.

Chase watches us—his face unreadable and then open at the edges—and rests his forearm against mine like an offering. I find myself skirting two futures: the steady shelter of him, the warm, dangerous flicker of Sam who keeps appearing in weathered T-shirts like a possibility that burns bright and fast.

At night, when the ward quiets, I patch the small edges together with counting and breath and the skill in my hands to make cups of tea for bleeding hearts. Emily sits across from me, apron folded into a neat rectangle on her lap; she catches my eye and presses her lips together, the little secret smile she keeps for the wrong moments. She's hiding something the way people hide joy and terror together: in the hollow of her mouth, a new concern and a budding, shy possibility. I see it in the way she holds the sugar packet—like a small, precarious hope.

Outside my curtained bed a silhouette passes—Mr Rowan, polite, with the kind of professional voice that smooths edges. He says something to Charlie about a line in her drawing and Charlie's eyes go soft with the rare pleasure of being seen. Rowan's help feels like a mercy at first: he listens, he offers a bit of art supply, he gives a small compliment and leaves. To Charlie it's a beacon; to me it's a detail I tuck away like a pebble I'll later use to build an argument for unease.

I hold Rosaleigh and count tiles and breathe until the world becomes a geometry I can live inside. Waiting is still a fight you do lying down—but it is also a place where people show up in small, steady ways. This time, I am not alone.

Chapter Twenty-One

Three Days of

Silence

The procedure doesn't sit neat in the lines surgeons draw. Some wounds hide in charts and some keeps its teeth.

Somewhere between extraction and recovery my blood pressure plummets. The alarms that used to be background—soft punctuation to the ward—suddenly scream. Voices sprout orders and answers and the kind of panic that remembers to be useful. Then the world slides sideways and blankets itself in black.

They call it a coma. It's sleep with the volume dialled down and the past cued on repeat. I lie in a room with no doors; two nights splice themselves together until the seams burn. Rain needles a windscreen. The seatbelt arc at my collarbone bites. Mum's lemon-clean hand reaches and reaches and then headlights bloom too-bright. The other reel skates in: bar light, metal, the yank on my ponytail. I try to scream and my voice is a fish on tile. I try to run and the floor is glue.

From somewhere out there real hands and voices lean in and fog the glass.

"Cas. Back to me, duck," Emily says, fierce and even when her voice breaks. "Follow my voice."

"With me, Bitesize," Chase says, slow and low. "In four. Out six. Count with me."

Sam is rough with regret: "I'm sorry for every year I didn't—just… stay."

Charlie, thin and raw and unbelievably small, says, "Please, Cas. Please come back. I can't do the corridors without you."

I claw for the sound and it tugs me, like a line thrown into dark water. They call again; I answer. The anchors refuse to let my mind float free.

Outside, life continues in the implacable way hospitals have; the corridors keep happening. Charlie refuses to leave the room even when Jesse ushers gently and Emily pleads. She grips my hand like a talisman. Jesse and Sam nearly come to blows in the hallway—two different terrors trying on the same armour. Emily separates them with a look that is more mother than manager and the rift hums anyway.

At the lift alcove Amelia corners Chase with perfume like a dare. "She's already gone," she says, syrup on steel. "You can't be a martyr forever. The bar needs you. I need you."

"I'm not discussing this with you," he answers, voice so quiet it cuts.

"She dies and you still choose her," Amelia whispers, teeth glittering. "It's pathetic."

Emily arrives from nowhere. "Leave," she tells Amelia, quiet but hard. "Before I forget I'm wearing a visitor badge."

Amelia laughs like glass and glides away. Chase leans his head against the wall for two breaths, then returns to my chair and starts the counting again.

On the third night a real alarm goes— faulty wiring in a supply closet, smoke that shouldn't be. For a moment the false alarms and the internal ones all blur together until they are one shape, screaming.

In the clouded half-light I feel the shove of air change. Charlie's fear spikes and finds the last steady thread in me. I wrench upward.

Light knifes in. Grey haze fingers the ceiling; the monitor scolds. Tape rips. Lines pull. Pain snaps along my hips where bone gave what bone could give. I swing my legs to the floor and the bed rail punches my hip— anchoring me. The floor holds.

"Charlie," I rasp.

The door resists then opens. Smoke claws at my throat. In the corridor a nurse moves like choreography and trucks wheel by like a small tornado of clinical calm. Someone shouts numbers. Something heavy drops and the sound it makes is a word I won't say.

There she is—pressed flat against the wall, lungs testing air like an examination—and I call, "Here. With me."

I bend, make my body a roof. "Low. Breathe through your shirt," I say. In four, out six, ragged as a prayer.

We crawl. A nurse appears like a miracle and shepherds us into the stairwell where the air tastes like an honest slap. We land on the concrete step and the world is two small, furious people: me and her.

"Cas—" Charlie sobs now she has room for sound. "You came back."

"Always," I whisper, forehead to hers. "Every time."

Adrenaline drains. Hands lift her away; other hands lower me to a bench. The wall is cool. I let dark take me again—softer this time, like a blanket.

When I surface, antiseptic slices the air and the machine beeps are polite. My throat is raw.

"You scared the shit out of us," Emily says. She tries to laugh and it comes out half-sob. Mascara ghosts under her eyes. She looks like a woman who has eaten an entire night and is proud she didn't throw up.

"Charlie?" I ask.

"She's fine." Emily's hand is already on my arm. "Because of you. The sprinkler worked. Wrong closet, right system. You woke up into it. Of course you did."

Sam appears, pale and haunted, glad to be more useful standing than regretting. "They said you might not wake," he says. "I thought I'd lost you."

Chase folds into the doorway, voice steady. "The marrow's viable," he tells us. "They've started. It's a waiting game."

Jesse hovers, softer than he sounds. "You're reckless," he says. "But right."

When Charlie stirs on the edge of the bed, the first thing she says breaks open something in me. "You came back."

"Always," I say.

"You scared me."

"I scared myself," I laugh weakly. "But I'd do it again. For you."

She folds into me and for a long minute, I let the world be what it wants: a place where someone else's life can fit in the palm of my hand and not fall through.

Later, when the room quiets, the murmur from the coma hangs in the corners. But now there are anchors: Emily, Chase, Sam, Jesse, and Charlie. I survived the harvest; I survived the fire. I lay a palm on the old seatbelt arc and breathe, one… five… one, until the ward sounds like tide again.

Charlie's POV: Smoke Signals

Hospitals make you learn how to sit. You have to breathe in a way that doesn't annoy nurses and keep your knees where chairs think knees belong. Emily handed me a hot chocolate and said, "Sip," like it was a verb that could save us.

They took Cas to theatre. It's funny they call it that. No one claps. No one bows. They said, "Two hours. Maybe three." Time became a rubber band I snapped on my wrist.

Mr Rowan texted: *Here if you want noise that isn't hospital.* He's my favourite teacher because he doesn't call me Charlotte and because he keeps pencils sharp. He says lists save lives. *Write around the hard bit,* he says. *You don't have to write through it yet.*

When the fire alarm started, I thought it was my head making the hospital louder. Then a nurse said, "This isn't a drill," in a voice that made the words heavy, and I stood up so fast the chair complained.

Smoke curled under the door at the end of the corridor like a cat that didn't belong to anyone. Everything went fast and slow together. A man shouted room numbers. A woman pushed two wheelchairs at once. I wasn't supposed to be in the ward yet but I was, because rules evaporate when your person is behind a door.

I saw her before she saw me—gown crooked, wires loose, eyes too bright for someone who'd just had something taken out of their bones. She bent around me like water and said, "Keep low," and covered my head with her hands like I was a candle in a wind.

We crawled. A ceiling tile fell and sounded like a plate with a history. The air in the stairwell hurt like it was good for you. I cried so hard I couldn't tell if I was breathing right. She touched her old seatbelt scar and counted. In four. Out six. I did it too. We matched.

Outside, a nurse said words like *contained* and *faulty wiring* and *lucky*. Emily showed up like a small, pretty hurricane and wrapped me in a blanket that smelled like a clean hotel. Jesse put his hand on the back of my head for exactly three seconds and it was the best three seconds of the day. Chase didn't look at me. He looked at the building like it had personally offended him.

After, Mr Rowan sent a photo of the school courtyard in rain and wrote: *Two breaths on the bench, then one step. Works here too.* I didn't answer, but I breathed like he said. Two. One.

They took Cas back to a different room with less smoke and more beeping. Someone said *engraftment* and *day zero*. I said nothing and stood very still because that's how you keep from falling apart when your person has done something brave and stupid and necessary.

When they finally let me in, she was sleeping sideways again, like she'd left a space my shape. I climbed in, carefully. She woke up enough to say, "Always," like a promise and a warning.

I believed her. I believe her now.

Interlude — Amelia & Eli: Two Small, Complicated Hands

Eli's first week out of hospital is a mess of apologies, mornings pretending to be worth something, and the kind of shaky phone calls you make when you are ashamed of the person you were.

Amelia shows up at Unit 3 the day the doctor lets him out: not with a swaggering entitlement but awkwardly with a thrift-bought hoodie (neutral grey, a tiny burn at the cuff), a paper bag of clean socks, and a face that looks like someone trying an experiment in being human. She stands outside his door for more than a minute, taps the frame, then goes in with her spine straight. People who work in edges of things sometimes surprise you.

She brings coffee. She doesn't offer flippant lines. She sits on the edge of the bed—no chair ceremony—and folds her hands like a shape that is uncomplicated and sincere for a second. Eli's grin is fragile, then real. "You didn't have to," he says.

"You did," she replies, and there's no silky cruelty in it. "Someone had to show up. And someone had to stop you from doing the dramatic hero thing again." It's blunt soft care. He laughs too loud, embarrassed. She gives him the hoodie with a single look: "Wear it." There's something like kindness in the set of her mouth.

It's small, and it confuses everyone who's catalogued Amelia as a blade. Jesse watches from the doorway and tilts his head. Emily buys it on principle of seeing someone doing better. Chase nods once like it's evidence the world is complicated.

Eli folds the hoodie over his knees like it's a talisman and later tells me, "She… didn't make sense. But she did something." He is not sure whether to be grateful or suspicious, and the mix of both makes him more human than he's been in a long time.

Amelia's softness is not redemption written neat. There are lines in her face that could still be barbed. It's just—today—a hand that offered socks and didn't ask for a return. That's enough for Eli to breathe once without tasting guilt.

Chapter Twenty-Two:

A Note, a Request,

A Gaze

On a slow afternoon, tucked between physio visits and the small bureaucracy of hospital food, a message comes in on the ward iPad: an email from Mr Rowan. He signs as "Martin Rowan — Arts Facilitator, Children's Program." His tone is careful and plain. Ms Patel recommended I might like a room with paper, he writes. He also offers, politely, to run a short art session at Charlie's school — a single class, exploratory, "just to get kids drawing again," with parental and school permission. He includes a professional reference from the hospital's child-health volunteer co-ordinator and a line that reads: If you think it might help Charlotte feel safer, I'm happy to coordinate with Ms Patel.

The ask is small and seems generous. Charlie lights up when I show it to her—she calls him the teacher who doesn't call her Charlotte—and for three days the email lives in the soft place between hope and the world's ability to break things.

One afternoon, sitting by the window with a cup of tea that tastes of hospital plastic, I notice him in the corridor reflected in the glass: a tidy man with grey at his temples, calm hands, and eyes that find my sister's line drawing stuck to the board outside her bed and hold on it the fraction of a second too long. There is nothing in the way he looks—no smile, no overt claim—but something in that fraction presses against a muscle in my chest and makes it twitch like a remembered throb.

I try to name it. I tell myself I am tired. I tell myself the brain is a lousy witness when it's exhausted. I think about the looping of

nightmares and the way faces sometimes

behave like echoes. I write down the moment

on the back of a card and tuck it into my

pocket. I walk to the ring of the ward and

count: four in, six out.

When the idea occurs to me—maybe Mr

Rowan shouldn't be allowed near Charlie

alone—I almost say it out loud to Chase in the

corridor. I practice the words: He seems nice,

but his eyes — but it sounds insane when I put

it together. Paranoia has a particular timbre. I

have heard it used to silence people before. I

think of Sam's return, of the marinade of lies

that made things worse, and I feel the tug of

wanting to protect Charlie by making louder

alarms. I feel the equal and opposite tug: don't

squander the thing that might make her feel seen.

In the end I tell Chase a partial truth. "Ms Patel told him about the ward," I say, voice small. "He wants to run a session. It could be good."

He watches me, scanning my face like a map. "You think it's fine?"

I look at my hands. "I don't know," I say. "Sometimes I feel like I'm inventing alarms."

His reply is patience. "Then we do it together. We go to the first one. We don't leave her alone with him." He does not roll his eyes; he offers a rope. My disbelief settles into something steadier. Maybe I am not losing it. Maybe the world is complicated and we will make our own rules.

When Mr Rowan follows up with a polite phone call to Ms Patel asking about timetables I find myself watching the phone more than listening to the schedule. In the small, private places of my head a seed of unease grows a fraction. I tuck it away in the same pocket as the other notes and decide to keep my mouth shut until I either have reason to speak or stop feeling like I've been pulled taut.

For now, Charlie is hopeful. For now, Mr Rowan is kind in ways that are easy to explain. For now, the smallest terror is only a suspicion at the back of my throat. I choose to walk the fine line between protecting and smothering and let the people who love us both step into the light beside me.

Ms Patel's classroom smells like charcoal and glue and ten thousand tentative starts. The room is bright in that school way that pretends everything will be fixed by markers and library overdue fees. Charlie sits at the centre table, a ribbon at her sleeve, a sketchbook open like a shield.

Mr Rowan arrives with a carrier bag of paper, a box of blunt pencils, and the kind of smile that seems to have been practised in front of a mirror until it learned how to be casual. He introduces himself to the class in the kind of voice that doesn't ask permission to be gentle. "We're going to draw the noise today," he says. "Sound you can see. Sound you wished you could take back. Sound you'd like to keep."

The exercise is simple — close your eyes, remember a sound, draw it without words. It sends the kids into a quiet I haven't heard in months: heads tilt, tongues push at teeth, hands begin to shape. Charlie's hand moves like it has an instruction manual. She draws piano teeth and glass-wings and a small rabbit that looks like it's been patched a hundred times and still refuses to fall apart.

Mr Rowan kneels at her table without leaning over. He doesn't crowd the page. He asks, "What colour is that first sound?" He listens like it won't cost him anything. Charlie says green, and he nods like green is a wise answer and not a test.

He helps another boy translate a laugh into a row of crooked suns. He traces a circle in the air when a girl can't find the right line. He hands out green pencils like he knew to expect that colour in advance. There's a rhythm to him — a professional calm — that makes teachers relax; Ms Patel smiles more than once like she's collected a favor.

When the session ends and the kids disperse, Rowan asks Ms Patel whether he can run a weekly after-school club. "Kids get tired of talking," he says. "Paper lets you lie down with your thoughts and not have to say them." Ms Patel's answer is immediate and eager. "We could put it in the program," she says. "You'll have space Monday afternoons."

Charlie looks up at the prospect and something changes in her face — soft, hopeful. For the first time in weeks she tidies the edges of her drawing like it's a thing she can present to someone other than me. I feel a prickle, a small thing that wants to be either relief or alarm and refuses to decide.

When Rowan stands and collects his bag, his movement misses nothing. For a second his eyes meet mine across the room. The look is polite and quick, a professional nod. But beneath it something flickers — precise and small, like a camera shutter. I feel it the way you feel ice break under your foot: not yet a fall, but the sound of a faultline.

I tell myself I'm exhausted. I tell myself hormones and hospital hours and adrenaline strikes produce private alarms that don't mean anything in public. I tell myself a hundred other things because the alternative is to hold onto that look and name it, and naming feels like the beginning of a fight I don't have enough breath for.

Charlie comes back to my side with a safe, small grin. "He gave me a sketchbook," she says. "He said I could borrow his office when it's loud." The words land like a tiny gift. I take them as such and tuck the prick of discomfort into my pocket and count until it numbs.

I'll go to the first session. I will sit in the doorway with my hands folded into a human cage. I will watch. I will not be the woman who screams at shadows without reason. I will bring an anchor: Chase. I will let the world test itself under bright light instead of letting a glint in a face grow teeth in the dark.

Interlude: Chase's POV— Three Rows Back

He's not a teacher. He's not a counsellor or a social worker. He runs a bar, prints schedules, and breaks up fights involving sticky floors and too much bravado. But anyone who owns a building knows the architecture of safety: gates, sightlines, a person at the door.

I come to the school because Cas asked me to. She asked like someone asking for a favour and meant it like someone asking for backup. I take the back row. Two rows in front of me, she sits like a statue whose stones are softening—shoulders down a fraction, a hand on Charlie's knee as if to say I am here.

Rowan runs the room with trained hands. He sets paper like offering plates, rolls coloured pencils to a child who looks like he hasn't had a toy since the last census. The kid's face melts into a circle when Rowan explains that sound can be drawn. It's performing a magic trick — making the inner world visible — and the man does it well.

Then the man's eyes find Charlie. Not his whole face; not a political survey—just that tiny corner of a face where a child's guard lives. And he watches longer than any teacher needs to for the simple purpose of marking a student's progress. It's the wrong kind of watching. It is the look you use when you're cataloguing a thing you want to keep.

Something in my gut tenses. You train for stuff like this. You learn the small signals: the lag in a smile, the hand that softens at a child's shoulder a breath too long. I don't stand. I don't make a scene. I don't want to spook anyone. I want to observe. That's my job tonight.

After the session, I'm also the one to meet Rowan by the classroom door. Manners first—because I am a professional and this is a small, public negotiation.

"You've done this before," I say, because Incidental Truth is the easiest way to begin. His response is to tilt his head and say, "I used to run community workshops. I like helping kids find their place to be noisy on paper."

"Good," I say. "We're grateful. We'll likely attend the first one. We keep kids pretty visible. Safety in numbers, you know?"

He nods, polite, and for a country second his smile is a professional's card. He says, "Of course. The room is a public space. Parents are welcome."

"Parents will be there," I tell him without telling him everything I mean by that. "We'll keep Charlie in sight."

He's agreeable, too agreeable. I make a note: agreeable can be warm, or it can be the smile a man uses before he makes a ledger in his head.

Cas watches me as I talk, the way someone watches a hinge after learning it's not stuck. There is a question in her eyes that she hasn't said aloud: did I see something, or am I being made twitchy by the world? She breathes and gives a half-answer. I take her hand under the table and squeeze once. It's a quiet signal — I'm with you. We'll make it public.

I don't like the way his hand lingers on his bag as he leaves. It's a small strike on a bell. I file it away, along with dozens of other small things people tend to ignore. Memory is a stack of receipts. Put them in order; they'll tell a story.

For now, we attend the after-school club. We sit three rows back. We do not make him feel watched; we make the room loud with our presence.

After the Workshop: Quiet

Unsettling

The first after-school club is bright with crayons and quiet with the kind of attention children can only muster when an adult has given them permission. Charlie's cheeks are flushed when we arrive, as if she has been running in place with excitement. The teacher count, the sign-in book, the way Mr Rowan greets each child by name — all the rituals of organized safety.

He watches Charlie when he doesn't need to, then helps a younger child lace a shoe with a patience that makes me want to believe him. The session ends with parents hovering, exchanging forms and phrases. I linger at the door and watch as he folds the last sheet of paper into his bag. His fingers brush Charlie's drawing as he passes, and the contact is small—professional, maybe—but precise in the way a man who catalogues things would be.

Charlie sees him after she leaves. She runs an arm through mine. "He said I could use his office if I needed a quiet place," she says. Her voice is tentative with the newness of being chosen. I tell her that's good. I tell her that we'll come to the next one.

As we walk away, my chest tightens. I want to be the kind of person who trusts the world is mostly kids and paper and good intentions. I also know the architecture of patterns. The man's work is good enough to help him earn trust. The way he touches paper and people is expert. The way his eyes track a particular child for a chisel-long beat is not.

I keep both truths. I will not be the woman who destroys something for a child because she feared a shadow. I will not be the woman who ignores a tone because it is polite. I pick a middle course: visible presence, careful notes, an arrangement with Chase to attend when we can.

The seed of the unease is planted. It will need water to grow. I will watch it with my hands out to prevent it from taking root where it doesn't belong.

Chapter Twenty-Three:

The Song in Emerald

By afternoon the ward thermostat has a

fever too.

Machines blink polite lies; nurses move like

tides.

Through the glass, a tiny chest rises then

stutters then remembers itself.

Numbers climb, dip, claw back. *Engraftment*

is a process, the registrar said, and processes

are just fights that last longer than you want.

I leave a loop of green ribbon on the shelf

outside isolation—frayed, the colour of

rainlight through gum leaves. It's the same

ribbon Mum tied in her hair the night of the

accident, the same one Charlie wove into her

braid. Mine had been around my wrist; I

remember the knot snapping when the world

did. I smooth it flat now and tuck it beside the

visitor tag, a silent charm for the three of us who never made it home the same way.

For the first time in years, I put on my glasses.

The world sharpens so suddenly it hurts. I look like the girl I was before headlights and sirens turned memory into a fault line. Maybe that's why I took them off all those years ago — to blur the edges of everything that broke. Now, in this sterile half-light, clarity feels like rebellion.

When I catch my reflection in the observation glass, I almost recognise her.

Emily meets me at the lifts with a garment bag and a face that means *don't argue.*

"Two hours," she says. "You'll eat three mouthfuls, hear one speech, and pretend to enjoy cake. Jesse and I are here the moment anything tilts."

"I shouldn't go."

"You should breathe," she says, steering me into the lift.

"And Chase only turns thirty-two once. He hired a string quartet because he's dramatic; don't make me be the only one who notices."

The hotel ballroom glitters like it's auditioning for a richer life. Waiters slick by, trays balanced; crystal spits light. In a powder room that smells like roses and ambition, I fasten Mum's gold chain and step into an emerald dress that knows my edges better than I do. The same green as the ribbon. The same shade that once lived in the corners of family photos I can't bear to frame.

Chase finds me at the balcony doors, smoothing a cufflink that doesn't need help. Tux, tie loosened just enough, scars disappearing beneath the shirt but not pretending they never existed. He stops like someone pulled a handbrake in his chest.

"You clean up catastrophically well," he says.

"You're biased," I answer.

"Correct," he says, and doesn't touch me.

Amelia materialises at his elbow in a dress expensive enough to have opinions. "Green," she says, smile sweet as a bruise. "Bold."

"Traffic-light themed," I say lightly. "I'll stop when necessary."

Her smile curdles. "You should've stopped already," she murmurs for him alone. "She's a drowning pool. Let it go."

His jaw ticks. "We're done, Amelia."

She looks at me like I stole a thing she'd put a deposit on.

"We'll see," she says, and glides away — perfume sharp enough to sting.

Speeches happen—Emily's funny and true; Jesse's six words and better than all of them:

"Don't die. You owe us beers."

Laughter unknots shoulders. For a minute I believe in rooms without wrong doors.

Later, in a wood-panelled side room, a piano waits like a secret. Chase slides the bench back and looks at me like asking permission is a language he learned late but fluently.

"Teach me," I say, and sit.

His jacket hits a chair. He takes the left half of the bench, a breath away.

"Hands here."

He arranges my fingers in a soft C, narrating every touch—"I'm at your wrist," "I'm moving your third"—so the ghosts don't bite.

"Not playing," he says. "Finding."

He taps a slow heartbeat: one… five… one. My right hand answers; my left trails, then learns.

A shape unfurls—simple as a door that opens inward, brave as the step that follows.

"This is ours," he says, almost to himself. "Something you can carry when the room gets loud."

We circle it until my hands know the way.

"Name it," he says.

"Glass Wings," I answer before I can stop the truth. "They look breakable. They aren't."

We don't kiss. We don't have to. For five minutes and a lifetime, skin, breath, sound—everything finds the same key.

A knock snips the quiet. Amelia leans in, slow-clapping with two fingertips. "Adorable. Teacher's pet learns middle C. Come cut the cake."

On the balcony, planes stitch the night with white thread. My phone shivers in my clutch:

1 new voicemail — Eli.

The preview ghosts up:

I'm at Unit 3, 11 Harrow Street, Briarbank…
don't freak out…

I press save and tuck the hum away for
morning.

Back inside, when he plays one last piece
for the room, I sit with my fingers on my
knees and count one… five… one under the
noise until the ballroom sounds like ours
again.

When I catch sight of myself reflected in
the polished lid of the piano—emerald,
glasses glinting, a loop of green ribbon at my
wrist—I almost believe I can be more than the
wreckage.

For the first time since the fire, I look whole
enough to risk breaking again.

Interlude: Eli & Emerald

The morning after the first club, Eli is washing down the bar, humming a tune that sounds suspiciously like a cabaret number gone shy. He catches my eye and winks like compensation for last week's voicemail. There's a small lingering guilt at how messy he was the night of the overdose and how soft Amelia's voice softened into something like worry two mornings later. People change in little increments and sometimes kindness is exactly messy enough to be true.

He slides me a napkin with the word EMERALD underlined three times. "I thought about the colour last night," he says. "More like a soft scandal, like a green that's apologetic but still makes an entrance."

"You're a poet," I say, which earns me one of those smiles where it's obvious the person is trying not to cry and failing in the best possible way.

He plays at words until the bar feels like an instrument tuned just right. The small levity is medicine. Amelia buys him a coffee later and tells him, quietly, "Don't make me have to collect you." Her tone is hard but not cruel; it is the kind of softening that looks like a rescue in practice, and it throws him off-balance in a way that makes him human.

We all could use a little human.

Detective Noor — Case Notes

Subject: Take Flight aggravated assault (female, 23), subsequent threats, and related fire/lock events.

Lead: D/S Noor.

Status: Active—offender at large.

- **Victim ID:** Cassianna "Cas" ________. Initial statement taken in hospital (see audio file DN-24-A). Follow-up pending when medically appropriate.

- **MO from victim:** Male offender with **green eyes** ("bottle-glass"), **thin lightning-nick scar** above right brow. Ski mask. Entered via **rear service door** shortly after close. Knife to throat; threats NOT monetary. Severe lacerations to rib/thigh; attempted escalation interrupted by staff response. Offender fled down stairs when confronted; cut across Jesse ______ (security) with blade. Exit path unknown.

- **Scene:** Back corridor shows repeated **scrape marks** on latch plate. Door had known **latching faults** prior to assault; **locksmith installed new bar + deadbolt** on Wed (invoice attached). Post-repair tests confirm solid engagement—requires deliberate force to rattle. CCTV coverage **insufficient**: existing camera grid leaves **blind cone** at bottom third of stairwell and **alley mouth** beyond bins. Recommend additional units + motion flood.

- **Witnesses (key):**

- **Emily** _______ (manager): corroborates door issues; notes **Amelia** _______ frequently behind bar w/o staff status; observed giving **Eli** _______ alcohol ("shots in glass washer"), prior to incident night; reports Amelia hostility toward victim.

- **Jesse** _______ (security): confirms **deliberate handle rattle + metal-on-metal** scrape night before assault; describes offender's movement as **trained/decisive**; believes offender familiar with layout.

- **Chase** _______ (owner): verifies back-door history;

engaged **after-hours training** with victim (basement gym); present at incident; tackled offender on landing; **offender strong, approx. 180–185 cm.**

- o **Eli _______** (bartender): inconsistent timeline; late arrival shifts; observed intoxication; VM to victim **02:11** ("Unit 3, 11 Harrow St, Briarbank") requesting hoodie + not to inform management. **Follow-up required.** Warrant prep if non-cooperative.

- **Other links:** Prior **vehicular collision** involving victim's family (old overpass); two separate witnesses recall **green-eyed male** loitering near

Take Flight days prior; victim previously reported being **followed** (see DN-22-MISC). Potential fixation offender.

- **Hospital fire:** Faulty supply-closet wiring; **sprinklers contained.** No evidence of arson at this time. Noting coincidence with victim's post-op **coma**—woke during alarm; escorted minor (Charlie ______) to stairwell. Interviewed three staff; nothing suspicious.

- **Action items:**

0. Pull **street CCTV** near **Harrow St, Briarbank**. Verify occupants Unit 3. Cross with **green-eyed male, possible scar.**

1. Trace **Amelia** _______ movements day
of assault; review interactions w/ Eli; check
outgoing **payment logs** and rideshare.

2. Dump phones (with consent/warrants):
victim, Eli, Amelia.

3. Forensic swabs from victim **under
nails** (logged); knife trajectory suggests
offender **left-hand dominant**.

4. Re-canvas alley businesses; look for
glove/knife discard in drains.

5. Safeguard measures at Take Flight:
panic pedal, auto-chime on back door, staff
buddy walk protocol.

- **Note (personal):** Victim displays
  trained breathing pattern under stress
  ("four in, six out"). May be key to
  anchoring during long interview.
  Return when medical clears. Offender

likely to escalate. Advise protective detail on closing nights until arrest.

Pre-Chapter Interlude A — After-School Gate

The first time I actually see him outside school, it feels like an accident.

Charlie has been hanging back by the bike racks — the ribbon at her wrist catching light — while I argue with the stern receptionist about parking for a minute too long. When I round the corner he's there by the noticeboard, folding a flyer like he belongs to the building. He looks up and offers the practiced smile again.

"Mr Rowan," Charlie says, and his voice is the careful kind kids use for adults who smell like authority and coffee. "Hi."

He crouches a little to match her height. "Good to see you outside the art room, Charlie. I was just leaving — brought those extra green pencils for next week." He hands over a small packet with fingers that don't fumble. It's a small gift: plausible, thoughtful.

I watch him watch her watch the packet open. He knows the exact way a child will unwrap something; he times the gesture so that the moment looks like belonging.

"Thanks," she says, smiling at a better width than she's allowed at the canteen.

He straightens, and for a beat his gaze grazes mine. There's a polite nod, and the man says, "If you ever need a quiet desk, the office is free Monday afternoons." Public. Open. Helpful.

I like that he is visible. Visibility is my friend. But the way he remembers which seat she prefers — or says it back to her later — leaves a residue. Small details grow roots if you give them water. I make a note in my head and tuck it with the other things I will watch.

Pre-Chapter Interlude B — The Green Ribbon Detail

A week later, Charlie bursts in like a summer storm and hands me a folded scrap of paper with the edges already soft from being turned over in small fingers.

"Look," she says. "He knew the ribbon colour." Her voice scrapes with confusion and the kind of hurt that calls itself curiosity first. "He said 'green ribbon' like he's seen it before."

I stare at the doodle she gives me. It's a small sketch — a sliver of cloth tied into a knot, drawn clumsy and fierce. The line isn't about a rabbit. It's about a colour.

"She said it during class," Charlie adds. "Like he remembered a thing from once."

My throat goes cold in the familiar way

— the seatbelt notch above my collarbone —

a memory that fits too well. That ribbon is not

just a colour; it's a small private map.

Evangeline had tied it in the corner of her

scarf the night of the accident. I had it at my

wrist. Charlie had hers knotted into a plait.

We all wore the green that made noise like an

inside joke. The sight of it is a slice of a night

I kept folded and put away.

I say nothing that sounds like accusation.

Instead I fold her paper and slip it behind my

phone like a talisman, because the least

violent thing to do is watch, not accuse.

Thin Ice

The numbers look good until they don't.

"Early engraftment," the haematologist says, tapping a chart that might as well be a star map. "Counts are rising. That's what we want." Sam exhales like he's been holding his breath since the car park. Relief lands warm between my shoulders—and then, because joy never arrives alone: "Watch for fever, rash. It can flip fast."

Thin ice. Smile, don't jump.

I sit with Rosaleigh and her rabbit while cartoons warble. When she wakes, she blinks up like I've always been here. "Mum," she tests, small and certain.

The word carves itself open and I answer it with everything I am learning how to be: steady, present, not disappeared.

Sam finds me in the family room with two lemon teas from a machine that thinks kindness is temperature. He doesn't step too close. "Thank you," he says, voice frayed. "For… all of it. If she lives, it's because you gave her back to the world."

"We both brought her here," I answer. "As kids. As idiots. As parents, eventually." I try to smile. It holds for three seconds.

We go to the cemetery at dusk the next day because grief learns ritual. Rain makes the gravel smell like crushed paper. We kneel at the stones and ask a question we should have asked long before: Why was I told to carry a body when the body lived?

"Maybe they thought they were saving you," Sam says, fingers cold on granite.

"Maybe the town thought it made more sense to bury a story until someone else dug it up."

I tie a green ribbon around a low fence post on the way out because a thread is better than forgetting.

Back home, the quiet is too loud. I go where noise can be guided: the hidden gym. The bag is an honest instrument. The first night I return I tape my hands, the elastic of the wraps whispering resolve.

Jab. Cross. Hook. The rhythm breathes out the panic. The world reduces to a sequence you can count. And for an hour it's enough.

Jesse leans in the door like he owns the doorway this week, chin tucked. "You're running hot," he says.

"I'm fine," I say.

"You're vibrating like a line," he says. "You want to talk about almost losing her, or almost losing Charlie, or Sam… pick one."

Later, Eli slides in like a shadow that's decided to matter. He smells faintly like a night he'd rather not relive but is reliving anyway. There's a new softness in him — Amelia's attention has complicated whatever path he was on; she's softened in ways that look less performative and more tangled. That complexity of kindness and danger sits on him like a jacket.

"Pads?" I toss him a pair. We work light. He flinches at too much contact. He jokes to mask terror. Once, between rounds, he leans against the ropes and breathes words about emeralds and pages and mint ice-cream. He's

trying to trade language for sobriety and
sometimes it works.

Halfway through the session, a knock at
the back door—three quick, two slow. Jesse's
face goes flat. "Don't," he says.

Nothing comes in, just the echo of a
rhythm on metal. It's enough to remind me
why doors get new bolts.

On the tram home a text pings: Open
spar, cash. No questions. Tonight. The city
slides past like a film reel. The invitation is a
door I've walked through before with bad
intentions: underground fights, cheap rules,
clearer pain. The ache in my bones answers.

That night I don't run. I lace gloves and
breathe until the seatbelt notch above my
collarbone calms. I call Chase and ask for a
round in the proper ring. He says yes, quiet

and immediate, and the simplicity of his yes feels like a rescue.

At the end of the week, a small, private complexity blooms in the bar: Amelia's hand hovers at Eli's shoulder with a care that isn't all show. She brings him coffee without it being photographed. When a late night they share a cigarette behind the dumpster, she presses her palm to his back like someone trying to steady a kite string. The gesture is not an absolution; it is a human mess.

That night, under a streetlight, I wonder whether she's softening because she's learned fear, because she likes him, or because she's trying to buy something that wasn't hers to own. I tuck the thought away for when I have time to catalog motives.

What I do not tuck away is the ache that buys an entrance into a different life: Sam's face when Rosie calls him "Dad," Charlie's small hands in mine, and the echo of a bell in a warehouse that still makes my blood hum.

Chapter Twenty-Five

The First Bell

The warehouse smells like rust and river and cheap aftershave. Fluoro lights make a flat white ring around the taped square. People lean on pallets, count cash, hold their breaths.

A woman with a lavender bruise under one eye sizes me up. "You here to watch or make rent?" she asks, the way someone checks whether you belong to their circus.

"Neither," I say. "I'm here to breathe."

She smirks, tosses me gloves. "Two three-minute rounds. No heads. No biting. Most of the rules you break are the ones that keep you alive."

I write Bitesize in chalk on my mind because Chase calls me that and because the name fits better than anything I invented for myself.

My opponent is rangy, long-armed, looks like trouble shaped into a human. He moves fast. He hits faster. Each impact is an arithmetic of pain — subtract, count, adjust. It's ugly. It's useful.

By round two, he clips my ribs and the world skews. I taste iron and panic. Somewhere ahead smoke smells like hospital memory and Charlie's voice—Don't you dare die—threads through the noise.

I hit back and something in me hushes. When his guard drops, I land the hook that matters. He flounders; the crowd makes a noise that could be applause or relief.

A woman calls time by slapping concrete. She grins at me like I passed an exam. "Back next Friday," she says.

I stand in the cold outside the warehouse and breathe until the adrenaline drops enough to leave a bruise. That's when Chase steps out from the shadow like a man who has been pacing a line and knows exactly where to stop.

"What the hell do you think you're doing?" he asks. The anger is real but artistically controlled.

"You're bleeding," he says more plainly. "You can't afford this."

"I can breathe here," I say. "I can make the noise small enough to take back."

"You can breathe where I can keep you standing," he replies. His voice is a handrail. "We made rules. We made a ring. No vans, no back alleys. Earn the fight, don't barter with your life in exchange for calm."

I nod because everything else would make the line between us spike. We don't argue into a shouting match; we have a map: the gym, the sanctioned sparring, cards if that is what I want. He will fight the idea of me fighting dirty — not because he doesn't think I can, but because he remembers a woman who nearly didn't come back.

The next morning there's a small birth of gossip across the bar. Amelia's laughter is quieter these days; she moves around Eli as if the space between them is warmer than before. No one pins a name to it, but I catch Amelia's hand at the little hollow between his shoulders one slow Tuesday, and the way she looks at him is not entirely possessive — it's complicated, like a person who both enjoys and fears being needed.

We take the public route forward:

sanctioned sparring, public booths, referees

with strict lists of fouls. I work in a lane of

pain that is observed, scored, and recorded.

Addiction to the rush doesn't vanish, but it

gains rules — and rules buy me back into

family calculation: Sam's quiet gratitude,

Rosie's small hand searching for mine,

Charlie's steady homework presence.

Interlude: Charlie's POV — Trust, betrayal and repair

When I found out Rosie had been alive, I stared at Mum and the wall and then at the calendar. For a while I believed that adults had a private language where they chopped pain into smaller pieces and called it mercy. I felt betrayed because the truth was like a missing stitch in a favourite sweater: suddenly the whole thing could come apart and no one told me how to sew.

For months I kept my distance in a safe way: I carried headphones even when I didn't listen because moving your mouth is harder than moving your feet. When Rosie arrived — small, stubborn, real — I felt something crack and then repair itself with pieces that weren't mine. I hugged Cas like I was anchoring a boat.

Now Cas is coming back from something big and dangerous and we both smell like the same smoke. I watched her sleep the night after engraftment and saw that her chest rose in the old counting pattern, that she'd learned to make space for the world again.

When she left for the fight at the warehouse that night, I felt the old betrayal bubble up — why would she risk this if we're only starting to be a family? She came back bruised and alive and she chose to be with me in public the next day, and that choice is a stitch.

Healing is slow and messy and also a thing with edges. Tonight she sits at the kitchen table doing Rosie's fractions, and every time she breathes I think — she came back. That's the first thing we needed.

Interlude B: Ambiguous Complications

On a quiet Monday, Amelia steps into the bar office with a hand at the small of her stomach and a deliberate air of industry. She passes Chase a folded napkin that reads: "Call me later." There's a shadow of something private; the hand that fidgets with the napkin beats like a tiny moth.

No one knows if the news is for Chase or someone else. Amelia's smile is practiced; she kisses the back of Eli's hand that evening like she's making a vow in a language only they understand. People will gossip — of course they will — and they will choose a story that satisfies them. For now, she keeps it tight-lipped and small.

Chase notices the napkin — he files it under "complications" and closes the drawer. The fact that he does not slam the drawer tells me everything we need: whatever truth arrives, he plans to meet it busy and calm.

Chapter Twenty-Six:

Stone & Second

Bell

Morning finds me back at the cemetery because I don't know where else to store the night.

Rain has rinsed the marble to bone. I brush water from Mum's name with my sleeve, then Dad's. The letters shine briefly before dulling again, like memory teasing permanence.

"I don't know why you did it," I tell the stone. "I'm grateful for the girl you raised. I'm furious about the girl you erased. Both are true. I'm going to find the paper that explains your lie and decide what kind of daughter I still get to be."

Sam joins me, coffees balanced, eyes raw in the way men hate to be seen.

"The nurse—Trish—the one from back then? Still works admin," he says. "Rowan gave me her contact. He told me not to break anything while we wait."

"Rowan always knows everyone," I murmur. The joke tastes like dust but it's still a joke. "We'll ask her."

We leave lemon-gum sprigs because some griefs deserve clean scents. The air smells like crushed leaves and the first note of rain.

On the way out my phone hisses: *Open ring—tonight.* Different pin, different warehouse. The message sits in my palm like a coin I don't want to spend and will anyway.

I last until midnight.

The second warehouse is colder, meaner. A bare bulb trembles over a taped square. Sweat, rust, and breath make their own weather. A woman my size but sharper steps in opposite me. Her eyes say *earned teeth*.

We touch gloves. The world narrows.

She's quicker. I take a jab that tastes like metal and instinct wakes—the hum that asks for pain as proof. Jab-cross-hook. Her counter drives the air from my lungs. I count—one-five-one—and find rhythm in the bruise. No bell, just blood; mine. The crowd claps, not kind but honest. I grin through the sting because I'm alive in a way that doesn't demand meaning.

Outside, wind off the river turns sweat to knives. My phone vibrates:

Sam: *Fever dipped. She asked for mint.*

Charlie: □ + 🖤 (rabbit with ribbon).

Then an unknown number again: *Unit 3, 11*

Harrow Street. Don't freak out.

Eli's address, the refrain of a bad dream.

I breathe until the river stops crawling

inside my ribs. Then I walk home toward the

life that still wants me.

Detective Noor — Case Notes

- Unsanctioned bouts confirmed at two riverfront warehouses; alias "Bitesize" logged on chalk board. No arrests—patrol arrived post-dispersal. Recommend contact for victim-safety intervention (risk of offender crossover).

- Harrow St, Briarbank: property manager lists **E. — current tenant; A. — previous (Amelia)**. Interview pending; cross-match with voicemail evidence.

- Contact initiated with Trish M., clinical admin, regarding "infant transferred" entry in historical records. Awaiting court order for full disclosure.

- Owner (Chase) reports growing conflict with Amelia; evidence of alcohol supplied to Eli during shifts. Possible coercive influence.

- Continue protective presence at Take Flight closing hours. Monitor underground venues for offender sighting (green eyes, brow scar). *Note: Victim displays increased risk-seeking behaviour consistent with trauma recurrence.*

Chapter Twenty-Seven

Rejection

Four days later, fever.

It starts shy—heat cupped at the nape of Rosaleigh's neck—then roars. A rash flares like fingerprints of someone invisible.

"GVHD is a spectrum," the haematologist says, calm and practiced. "Grade I–II skin. We caught it early. Steroids, antimicrobials. We adjust."

Rejection. The word punches two eras at once: this sterile room and the delivery ward no one admits I remember—lemon disinfectant, my mother's hand crushing mine, a nurse whispering *I'm so sorry* while someone carried the crying out of the room.

Sam's knuckles bleach white on the bed rail. I take the other side, talk nonsense—mint ice cream, debate trophies, clouds shaped like ships—because small talk is the only anaesthetic we can share.

Hours pass measured by drips and alarms. In the corridor, Charlie corners Sam. "If she dies," she says quietly, "I'll never forgive either of you."

"We're not letting her," he answers.

"You already did." She turns away before the apology can form. Emily follows, shoulders taut with sisterhood and exhaustion.

When I return from washing my hands raw, I nearly trip over Eli—folded on the floor, hoodie up, eyes glassy.

"Hospital floors fail hygiene," I tell him, sliding down beside him anyway.

He gives a weak laugh. "You got disinfectant for being a mess?"

"I'm certified in messy."

He looks at his hands. "Amelia called. Said there was a job. 'Good money.' It was a tab and a back room and a blackout. I think I lost a day."

"Do you need a bed?"

"No. Just… not Amelia."

"Good start," I say, and let the silence be kind instead of heavy.

When I finally step back into the room, Rosaleigh's fever has broken half a degree. She asks for ice chips. Sam exhales a prayer he doesn't name. I smooth the green ribbon at her wrist—retied by her own small hands— and whisper the count: one-five-one. She dreams in safety's language.

In the hallway I pass Amelia near the lifts, immaculate as always, perfume sweet as threat.

"You and your hero complex," she says.

"Think he'll choose you because you bleed prettier?"

The old shame lifts its head; I meet its eyes and keep walking. "No," I say. "He'll choose not being lied to."

Her smile cuts thin. "Everyone lies, sweetheart. Efficient men know that."

"Then find better liars."

I leave her with her reflection.

On the tram, city lights smear like memory. Pregnancy sneaks up in the glass— mint once made me gag; lemon still does; maybe there's another reason Amelia keeps touching her stomach lately. Chase's? Eli's? No one knows. Maybe she doesn't either.

I touch the seat-belt scar that borders newer stitches and breathe four-in, six-out until the thought unclenches.

Home smells like graphite and toast. Charlie's at the table sketching a boxing ring: high ropes, one stool, a girl too small but standing anyway.

"Numbers look better," I say.

"Good." She shades the corner darker. "Don't die in a basement."

My pulse skips. "What?"

"Jesse told Emily. Emily told me. Don't."

"I won't," I promise, the half-truth I can live with. "Not in a basement."

She nods, the tiniest surrender. "If you need to punch something, hang a bag on the balcony."

"That'll thrill the neighbours."

"Good," she says, smiling for real this time.

My phone pings: **Unit 3, 11 Harrow Street**—no text, just the address. My heart stumbles once, twice. Ghost, threat, or clue, I save it and don't reply. Last time an address dictated my fate, I lost a child.

Before bed I text Jesse: *Got the message.* He sends a thumbs-up, then: *know a ref.*

The thin ice still sings under us. But Rosaleigh sleeps deeper, ribbon loose around her wrist, and Charlie's pencil keeps moving—drawing ropes high enough to keep out the dark.

Tomorrow, six a.m., I'll stand on tape that says *CENTER* and learn how not to back up when a fist comes.

Hands up. Breath steady. Bitesize. One thing.

Then another.

Chapter Twenty-Eight

Time to Move On

The nightmare takes me by the throat. I wake wrong—eyes open, body mute. A weight pins my chest like an argument I can't win.

Moonlight turns the wardrobe into a man. The fridge hum becomes a MET call. Smoke I can't smell curls under the door.

I try to move and nothing answers. I try to breathe and the air arrives in needles. The bar door scrapes. He is here again—knife, breath, wool—except there's no knife and the wool is my blanket and my brain does not care. A piano plays one note that never resolves.

Move a finger, I order.

The old seat-belt arc burns like a flare. I lock my eyes on it and count inside the paralysis: one … five … one. The right pinky trembles;

the world cracks.

Air slams back in. I sit up too fast and the room tears. Charlie's door opens with the soft panic of someone who's run this drill before.

She climbs into my bed, blanket and all. "Count," she whispers.

I do. In four. Out six.

Glass Wings under the doona until the terror bleeds out.

We don't mention the coma or the drowning-sleep. We talk instead about whether a green ribbon is still brave enough for a rabbit. She votes yes. I agree because agreeing is oxygen.

By dawn my tea's cold and my hands finally unclench. Maybe survival isn't a miracle; maybe it's a craft.

Daylight builds routine around the wreckage.

Weekends, I sell display homes that smell like paint and new promises. *Ensuite, cross-breeze, north light*—incantations against chaos.

The nursery stage sets hurt. A cot. A neutral bunny. I straighten a blanket, let the ache walk through, don't let it stay.

Weekdays, I juggle school runs, bills, late-night story time to a child who is learning my name in the right tense. Structure blunts panic. Four a.m. still hunts me, but now I know how to sit with it—In four, Out six— until dawn is less a threat and more a clock.

Emily corners me over coffee. "You can't keep orbiting Take Flight like it owes you a ghost," she says. "Move on."

I nod, because she's right. But some nights I still walk past the old bar just to hear the silence around the piano.

I sell Mum and Dad's ute, buy Charlie a laptop fast enough for art wars and debate prep, and sign papers on a sensible hatchback with good brakes and no history that smells like blood. Four wheels. One future.

Charlie shines. Debate turns posture into armour. Someone calls her eyes "rare-pretty" and means it. Confidence begets confidence. Rosaleigh learns my rhythm—the green ribbon retied by her own fingers. Sam brings cucumber sticks instead of peas; together we're clumsy, new, real.

Chase drills footwork at dawn. Tape squares. Pivot. *Cut the angle, Bitesize.* His voice steadies more than caffeine ever could.

Amelia ghosts the edges of every room: perfume, laugh, late-night texts to Eli. Once she appears at the gym door just long enough to say, "He'll get bored of building broken people," and vanishes before I can decide whether I'm angry or relieved.

Emily demands a beach bonfire. Salt, driftwood, Jesse on guitar, the sky stitched with smoke. Charlie asleep on my shoulder before nine.

Chase arrives late, alone. Our eyes catch. Something unspoken settles. I look away first. The sea listens.

Time to move on, I tell the water. It doesn't argue.

A week later Emily orchestrates a girls' night. Hair, dress, laughter at the edge of real. The pub hums—sticky joy, live bass, safe noise. We dance until our shoulders forget to hunch. Outside, fairy lights hang low enough to believe in.

Chase waits in the alley, sleeves pushed, no Amelia. The look between us shortens the world. Then Emily loops her arm through mine. "Home," she sings, dragging me toward the curb.

In the Uber she yawns against my shoulder. "You like him."

"He's taken."

"Life's messy," she murmurs. "That's where it gets good."

At six a.m. he points at my stance. "Again." Tape. Breath. Geometry of staying upright.

My phone buzzes: *Unit 3, 11 Harrow Street.* I almost delete it. Instead I type *Not yet.*

Then I drive to work and tell strangers where the light will fall in their new kitchen, and where—if they ever buy a piano—it will sound best.

In for four. Out for six. Glass Wings in my pocket. One thing. Then another.

Detective Noor — Case Notes

- Electrical cause confirmed for hospital fire; no arson indicators. Victim self-evacuated minor. Note: high resilience, continuing risk behaviour.

- Sleep-paralysis episodes reported by family. Recommend trauma-focused therapy.

- Amelia —— maintaining irregular contact with Eli ——; suspected unlicensed "good-money" off-site work.

- Harrow St (current E., previous A.) flagged; police interest ongoing.

- Illegal bouts: alias *Bitesize* observed; patrols increased.

- Archive release authorised re "infant transferred" notation—pending retrieval.

Chapter Twenty-Nine

Blood Is Thicker Than

Water

The call comes mid-shift: Charlie, principal's office, altercation.

I drive faster than guilt.

She's on the vinyl couch, split lip, knuckles scraped.

"She called me a freak," she says. "Said Mum and Dad wouldn't want me."

Pain lands clean and old.

"You don't have to prove anything."

Three-day suspension, pamphlet on *restorative conversations* — bureaucracy for heartbreak.

At home she paces. "I'm not sorry. I'm not weak."

"You're not," I say.

"I'm not a kid."

"You're not either," I answer. "But let me catch up."

Silence stretches, then softens. "They don't take me seriously."

"Being grown is how you carry yourself when no one's clapping," I say. "On that front? You're ahead."

She folds into me, furious and forgiving all at once.

Later she reappears, kettle in hand.

"Sorry I yelled."

"Accepted," I say. "Being grown also means that."

Eye-roll. Peace treaty.

Dinner is quiet, but the silence hums with what's missing — all the birthdays we skipped or survived through. The years when cake would've felt like betrayal.

Sam finds me later, phone in hand, scrolling through photos I thought we'd deleted.

Rosaleigh in plastic wings. Charlie's grin with teeth too big for her face. Emily's arm around us, all sunlight and noise.

"She's missed a lot," he says.

"So have I."

He leans against the counter. "Maybe it's time to give her one."

"I don't know how to celebrate what's half-healed," I say.

"Then start small. Paper lanterns, not fireworks."

He means well. But that night, I can't sit still.

I run until my lungs turn to ash, then drive until the roads blur into silver. The city lights stretch like veins. I take turns too fast, chase the ache in my chest, chase the edge because stillness feels worse.

One night ends at a warehouse club.

Bass, strangers, a flash of green light that

makes my heart seize.

Someone offers me a drink; I don't take it.

Another laughs, touches my arm. I almost

swing. Instead, I leave, shaking, adrenaline

humming like prayer.

Eli's waiting outside *Take Flight* when I

finally return. He's leaning against the door,

cigarette unlit.

"Didn't think you were the running type

anymore," he says.

"Didn't think you were sober long enough to

notice."

He smiles, faint. "Fair. But I see you

burning up for the wrong reasons."

I almost tell him to mind his own redemption,

but he beats me to it.

"When Chase and Em's parents took me in, I thought they'd made a mistake. I was sixteen, angry, and stealing for sport. But they never asked me to change — just to stay."

He looks at me then, eyes clear. "Sometimes that's the fight. Staying."

The next day, I find myself at the kitchen table with Charlie and a notepad.

Sam drops off streamers, Emily texts cake options, Jesse offers the yard.

"We don't have to do big," Charlie says.

"No," I say, forcing a smile. "Just right."

So we plan — fairy lights, lanterns, maybe a ribbon or two.

Every line on the list trembles between past and promise.

The party isn't today. Maybe not this year.

But the planning feels like breathing again.

When she goes to bed, I sit at the table a

while longer, scrolling back through Sam's

photos.

Rosie's laughter caught mid-spin. Emily's

wink from behind a sparkler.

The ghosts don't fade; they flicker, patient.

I pour water, not wine.

Count breaths instead of bruises.

And when the nightmares come armed, I tell

myself:

Stay.

Just stay.

Charlie's POV — Lessons in Weight

Saskia cropped me out of the photo and the story.

I learned three things:

1. People clap for cruelty if it looks rehearsed.

2. A line can wound if you know where to place the dark.

3. Adults forget small doesn't mean harmless.

Mr Rowan didn't say *sorry* like teachers do. He said, "Put it somewhere it can't rot you," and showed me how to press charcoal until the paper remembers.

"Eyes are anchors," he said. "Let them drag the viewer where you want."

His eyes are green with a brown shard—

like a crack catching light. I didn't stare. I just

wrote *sunburst* in the margin.

Cas says, *Text me when you finish.* I do.

She replies, *Proud of you.* It lands warmer

than when anyone else says it.

When I sleep, the ribbon is emerald and

the machines in the dream breathe steady.

I'm drawing a zine called *Thicker.*

Page one: a girl with two different eyes that

match on the inside.

Chapter Thirty:

Girls Just Want to

Have Fun

Emily declares a state of emergency in the mirror. "We are doing this properly," she says, barging in with armfuls of clothes, a tote full of makeup and a bottle of pink gin that sloshes like liquid bubble-gum. Charlie appears in the hallway, shark-curious.

"Not for you," Emily sing-songs, ruffling her hair. "Sister sleepover tomorrow. Tonight is adult chaos."

We turn the lounge into a dressing room: sequins and denim, a mess of clips, the smell of dry shampoo and cheap perfume. Emily tips my chin and wings my eyeliner into a kind of courage.

"I look… not like me," I tell the reflection.

"You look like you," she says, "but with the volume up." She holds a sparkly black top I would never buy. "Trust."

I fish a lime from the gin and put it back. Lime still remembers morning sickness. "No mint," I mutter. "Or lemon."

"Noted," she says, like a good bartender taking a new regular.

By the time the Uber pulls up, my nerves are an octave higher than the heels. Charlie watches from the doorway—half amusement, half careful. I blow her a kiss. "Tomorrow, pancakes."

"Not burnt."

"Negotiable," I say, and Emily hauls me into the night.

The club breathes neon. Bass lives in the floor and climbs bone. People shine like sweat is glamour. It smells of citrus peel and spilled beer and possibility. For a while the music does the talking; I remember that my body can be a place I like living in. Strangers offer drinks with smiles they imagine are irresistible. I shake my head and point at Emily because she's irresistible and already holding two cocktails and a lime wedge like props.

We collapse into a booth, breathless. "See?" Emily says, cheeks flushed. "You needed this."

She's right. The lightness isn't a betrayal tonight; it's a loan.

On the balcony, under fairy lights that turn cigarette smoke into lace, he is there— leaning against his car like it thought of him. No Amelia. Shirt sleeves rolled. Scars bright.

Chase's gaze finds me and holds, as if the world had chosen that spot hours ago.

He pushes off the door with the heel of his boot and closes half the distance, then the rest. "You look…" he starts, voice low with effort, "different."

"Good different or bad different?"

"Good," he says, simple. His eyes don't travel; they keep me. There is a note between us that hums close to something dangerous and something tender.

Emily knows weather. She loops her arm through mine. "After-party," she declares, hauling me sideways. I glance back; Chase watches, unreadable, a man remembering something before deciding what to do with it.

In the Uber, Emily sighs into my shoulder. "You like him."

Heat climbs, traitor-slow. "He's taken."

"Life's messy," she murmurs. "That's where it gets good."

At her flat we raid the pantry, melt cheese on stale corn chips, squeeze lime over the mess, call it dinner and eat it standing up. We laugh at nothing until my ribs ache in a way I prefer. Emily falls asleep mid-story with a hand in the bowl. I fold a blanket over her and claim the sofa—mascara smudged, feet sticky with dance floor confetti. For the first time in so long I get to be a girl with a friend, not a witness with a ledger. I sleep like the sun is a promise I can cash.

My phone buzzes at 1:13 a.m.—a message from Charlie I'd missed in the noise.

CHARLIE: Mr Rowan says I should apply 4 winter studios—Briarbank Arts. Sat morn crits. Can I?

CHARLIE: I'll be with Ms. Patel for the first one. Promise.

CHARLIE: Don't freak out.

Briarbank. The word pings off Harrow Street—the address that keeps circling. I type *We'll talk in the morning* and don't send the other half: I'm already freaking out.

Six a.m comes mean and on time. Chase points at my feet. "Again." The world narrows to tape on the floor and the geometry of not breaking.

After drills he holds pads and I find Glass Wings in my breath—one, five, one—until the static thins. He doesn't mention last night. I don't either. Between us that silence is its own kind of honesty.

On the way to the hospital I pass a wall of posters: Briarbank Winter Studio — Youth Intake. A logo I don't know. An address I do. Ink smells new. I take a photo because suspicion is a kind of preparation, and because love trains you to notice patterns you'd rather miss.

At the ward Rosaleigh asks for cucumber and draws a rabbit with two lopsided ears. Sam yawns around his coffee and thanks me for the party again like gratitude could be currency enough. We are pretending to be better people than last year. Mostly it works.

That evening Charlie sets four plates without being asked and launches into a lecture about chiaroscuro like she swallowed a textbook. She drops a line that hangs in the air after the cutlery settles. "Mr Rowan says eyes are anchors," she says casually. "He says people look where the light tells them." She adds, almost as an afterthought, "His eyes are weird too. Not like mine. Just… a shard."

A shard in green. The sight of it hits like a match—mask, knife, breath through wool and the eyes I swore I'd never forget: green with a brown lightning streak.

I don't let my face move. "Huh," I say, as if I'm learning recipes. "We should meet him."

"Soon," she says, already reaching for her sketchbook. "He's busy. And I'm fine."

"Text me when you finish," I remind.

"Obviously." Her grin is rare and unguarded. For a moment the house stows its knives.

When the dishes are done and the night dials down, I pull the music box from the wardrobe, wind the key, let the tune wobble once, twice. I press my palm over the X on my ribs and breathe to the beat until my skin learns it again.

Tomorrow I'll call Ms Patel. Tomorrow I'll google Briarbank Arts and Harrow Street and pretend I'm just a parent doing due diligence. Tomorrow I'll be reasonable.

Tonight I write a word on a sticky note and tuck it behind my licence where only I will see it:

Doors.

Swing twice. Hear the latch. Check the latch. Meet the people who have keys.

Chapter Thirty-One:

Splinters

The text arrives just after last bell.

CHARLIE: running late—Rowan asked me to help hang canvases for Ms Patel's show. I'll be with him and Ms P. Promise.

The promise buys me forty minutes of not pacing. On minute forty-one I'm in the car, chewing a fingernail I stopped owning at fourteen. The art room spills soft yellow into a corridor gone quiet. Ms Patel waves with a wire hanger between her teeth, grateful and unbothered. "Five more minutes," she sings. "She's genuinely helpful."

Through the door: Charlie on a step-stool, level in hand; Mr Rowan near her shoulder. Early thirties, paint under his nails, forearms nicked with old turps, the kind of quiet a classroom leans toward. When he laughs it's mostly breath. His eyes are green with a fracture—a brown sunburst near the pupil, lightning arrested mid-strike.

"Anchor lines," he says, showing Charlie where the eye wants to land. He doesn't touch her. He stands close enough to share heat. The speck in his right iris sits in the place my memory keeps returning to—another man, another night, a knife and wool and the same green catch. The memory arrives like salt and recedes.

I step in; he turns with the measured ease artists learn from too many ladders. "You must be Cas," he says, voice low, warm. "She's got an instinct for balance you can't teach."

"Lucky," I say, palms damp. "Thanks for staying back."

"Part of the gig." He nods at Charlie's level. "She's steadier than the seniors."

Ms Patel hops off a chair like gravity is a rumour. "He's saving my back," she adds, meaning the room is supervised, boxes ticked. "Ten minutes."

Rowan rummages in his satchel and produces a small sketchbook—good tooth, satisfying weight. "Here," he tells Charlie, casual as if casual could be taught. "Spare. Try sighting lines on trams. Don't show anyone until you're ready; people crowd a thing before it learns to stand."

Charlie's face lights. "Seriously?"

"Seriously." He grins; the shard in his eye flashes. *Artists hoard secrets until they're strong enough to be shared.* The sentence hangs like a nail.

"Ten minutes," I echo, and leave before my face says too much.

—

The night before the party, the warehouse finds me like a smell you can't stop chasing. I tell myself it's the last time—a valve bleed before fairy lights. Promises are elastic; mine snap.

Under corrugated iron the air is river-damp and stale with beer. Men in hoodies lean on pallets; women in puffers count notes like rosaries. The taped square is smaller than memory. It looks like a dare.

The shaved-head woman with the lavender bruise clocks me and grins like she knew I'd come back. "Two rounds. No elbows. No knees to the head. No dying." Someone's already written *Bitesize* in chalk.

My opponent is rangy, taller. He bounces like a man who learned speed so he wouldn't have to be careful. He tests with a lazy jab; I slip. The first real punch slams my ribs where bone remembers knives. Hot white blooms; my breath goes out like a light. I grin because the pain is clean.

Bag work leaks from bone into hand. Jab, cross, step. He doesn't move his feet; I file that away. Hook I didn't earn snaps my head; copper floods my mouth. I spit red and hear cheering like a storm rolling over a hill.

Left, right, hook—ugly and honest. He staggers. The circle tightens. Every strike is a purge: the scrape at the back door, the stairs, three days of nowhere while machines pretended to be heartbeats, smoke in Charlie's hair, a child whispering *Mummy* like a spell I didn't deserve to get back.

When he laughs his ribs open. I thread an uppercut where hubris made space; his eyes widen. It would be easy to finish. To be the person who finishes things. To give myself a different kind of scar.

In the strobe of light they stand there anyway: Mum, mouth open on a joke she never finished; Dad, hand on the wheel; Charlie, smoke-grey at the edges, eyes steady even when her voice shakes; a small girl with a rabbit and a green ribbon I keep tying because I can. The future crowds the ring; the past takes a step back.

My hands drop.

Booing comes like weather. He surges, script in hand. I could let him. Pain is easier than consequence.

Hands flood the ropes. One set is Chase's—hot, unambiguous. The other is Sam's—calloused, shaking. They haul me like a body from water.

"This again?" Chase's voice is sharp enough to cut the tape off my wrists. "When will you learn?"

Sam's eyes are wildfire barely contained. "Enough," he says, flat and desperate. "She needs you tomorrow. So does Charlie. Walk away."

The ref barks. The circle swears. Eli fights through bodies, pale and sweat-sick, eyes glassy but clearer than last week. "Car," he says. The look he gives me is disappointment laced with relief—like a brother uncertain if he can still be one.

We move—shoulders, curses, the stink of someone else's regret. Outside the river air is cold and clean; the moon a coin I don't deserve. Mint from a bystander's gum makes bile climb; old echoes come up like tide. I breathe until the wave passes.

"Not basements," Charlie had said. Jesse told Emily. Emily told her. I promised a version of truth that wouldn't make me a liar. Splinters collect in the soft places.

—

Morning: fairy lights snake a borrowed fence. My hands tremble threading wire, but bulbs hold. Charlie watches from the picnic table, suspicion shadowing her mouth. She doesn't ask. She ties balloons—three to a string—tight and decisive.

"Higher," she says. "Kids like the sky to look like a ceiling."

Jesse arrives with a grill that could sear a cow. Emily arrives with a whistle she doesn't need. Eli carries chairs, quiet, steady. Chase brings a DJ who wears a cardigan and sets the volume at thoughtful. Sam backs in with a cake too tall to be structurally sound and an expression that softens at the banner: *ROSALEIGH*—Charlie's handwriting, a one-eared rabbit sketched in the corner, the ribbon green.

By the time small guests arrive the yard hums. Sausages blacken in ways Australians insist are intentional. Fairy bread appears as if summoned. The cake leans and then decides not to. The sun hangs longer than forecast.

She stands at the gate like a traveller who walked into the wrong movie: rabbit clenched, eyes too wide. For a second she can't make the picture mean her.

I kneel so the world is level. "Happy birthday, snowflake."

It lands. Her mouth tips up. Her hand slips into mine like it belongs there.

When we sing she hides behind the rabbit, peeking to check the words. I help with candles; we make a wish too big for one throat. Smoke curls. She turns her face into my shoulder and says, small and clear, "Thank you, Mummy."

The word knits something that felt like it would always gape. It hurts in the right way.

"Always," I whisper into hair that smells like cake and clean shirts and a childhood that might survive.

Games that make no sense and all the sense. Eli judges musical statues like a magistrate. Jesse feeds people until they can't be sad. Emily herds small bodies like she was born on a whistle. Chase watches the gate and pretends not to see me tie and retie a ribbon like a sacrament.

Across the afternoon Charlie ghosts in and out—general in shorts—checking bins, righting chairs, sneaking her phone to message ROWAN a photo of the banner. He replies with a single word: *Composition.* Her smile is quiet and private; I file that away with the sketchbook in her bag and the shard in his eye.

As dusk settles we carry sleeping children to cars. The DJ winds cables. The banner breathes. The fairy lights click on like stars who want a closer look.

Chase meets my gaze over a dying grill. He doesn't come closer. He doesn't need to. The look says what's allowed: This is the fight I meant. Keep choosing it.

When the last bag is tied and the yard is ours I sit on the back step with dirty hands and sleeves hiding bruises that don't matter tonight. The door is open. The house smells like sugar and people. Inside, a girl I thought was dead breathes out candles in her sleep.

Splinters still live under the skin. They do not own the hand.

Interlude — Rosalie's POV: Seventh Birthday

Dad says I'm lucky because my blood knows how to find its way home.

That's how he explains it when people ask about the scar at my hip, the one shaped like a comma.

He says my mum gave me life twice—once the day I was born, and again when she gave me the part of her bones that tell other bones how to grow.

I like that version.

It sounds like magic the doctors forgot to name.

Sometimes people whisper that she was brave.

Other times they say the word *after* too softly to hear the rest.

When I asked what came after, Aunt Charlie
said, "Healing," like it was a place we all still
lived near.

The backyard smells like rain that hasn't
decided yet and sausages pretending to be
dragons.
Fairy lights blink in the trees, and someone
hung a banner that says SEVEN in letters big
enough to stand on.
Dad's voice keeps finding reasons to laugh,
like he's testing if the air will let him.
Mum smiles the way light bends through
water—shaky, beautiful, not quite sure if it's
supposed to stay.

I know the marks on her arms aren't
stories for me yet.
Charlie says bruises are just the body's way
of remembering too hard.

I don't understand that either, but I pretend I do because grown-ups like when you nod.

There's a green ribbon in my hair that keeps slipping.
Mum has the same one around her wrist, and Charlie wears hers like a secret woven into a bracelet.
It's the colour of leaves after rain—hope trying again.

When I was five, I lived in a world that didn't know how to pronounce her name.
When I was six, I learned my marrow came from someone called *Cas*.
When I asked Dad if Cas was short for castle, he said, "Something like that," and looked at the sky too long.
When she finally came, she didn't look like a castle.

She looked like a wish that had been folded and unfolded too many times, soft around the edges, still holding.

The cake has seven candles, white and plain, but Mum says white holds all the colours if you look long enough.
I believe her because her voice sounds like proof.
Charlie keeps the lighter away from me and says, "Safety first, jellybean," but her hands are shaking.
She always calls me that when she's nervous.
When I hug her, she squeezes so tight I can hear her heartbeat through her shirt.
It sounds like music from inside a shell.

Then the adults start using their whisper voices that are still somehow loud.
Dad's words come out clipped, like he's

scared of what's underneath.

Mum's voice tries to be calm but keeps

tripping.

Charlie holds me closer, tucking my head

under her chin.

Her hair smells like paint and toast and the

soap we both hate.

I listen through her heartbeat instead of

the walls.

If I stay very still, I can pretend the arguing is

thunder and we're camping,

and this is what it feels like to have a sister—

someone who doesn't need to fix the storm,

just keeps you dry until it passes.

When the shouting stops, the light feels

tired.

Mum comes outside again, smiling the kind of

smile you make out of spare parts.

Dad stands behind her like someone guarding

a flame in wind.

He touches her shoulder and she lets him.

For a moment, they look like people in the

middle of a fairy tale who haven't yet realised

they're the ending too.

She kneels in front of me and says,

"Happy birthday, snowflake."

The word *snowflake* is small and soft and

belongs nowhere near Australian summer,

but it fits me the way Bunny does under my

chin.

Her fingers brush my hair back, catching the

green ribbon,

and it feels like a story being rewritten from

the middle instead of the start.

I ask if bones remember each other.

She says, "Always."

I think maybe hearts do too.

Later, when the yard is glittered with crumbs and tired balloons, Charlie carries me inside, whispering something about how fast I'm growing.

I tell her she doesn't have to worry, because Mum's bones are in me now and that means we're both strong.

She laughs, but her eyes get shiny.

I pretend not to see.

When Dad tucks me in, Mum's shadow is still on the doorway.

I can tell because the air feels warm in a way that only happens when she's near.

Her ribbon glows soft in the light, a promise tied and retied but never broken.

I dream of a woman with bandaged hands

planting lights in the garden,

and each one grows into a candle that doesn't

go out,

no matter how hard the wind tries.

Each flame wears a green ribbon,

and together they make the night look like it's

learning how to heal.

Detective Noor — Case Notes

- Victim: Cassianna "Cas" [surname redacted].

- Bar assault: male offender; medium build; green eye with central brown "sunburst" in right iris; thin nick above right brow; left-handed knife wound pattern consistent with "X" across thorax.

- New locus: Briarbank Arts / "Winter Studio" intake posters; Harrow Street matches prior address left on victim's phone (Unit 3, 11 Harrow St, Briarbank).

- School art program: Artist-in-residence "Mr Rowan" (no first name yet). Observe iris.

- Underground fights: riverfront warehouses; alias "Bitesize" sighted; victim present; associates present (Chase K., Sam [surname redacted], Eli C.). Amelia V. noted as influence vector for Eli.

- Action: photo array with CHS staff incl. "Rowan (?)"; canvass Harrow St for CCTV; welfare checks on unit occupant(s).

Charlie's POV — Study of a Shard

Saskia shoved me at my locker. My lip tastes like coin. I could have swung. I didn't. Mr Rowan says force is just line with muscles; better to decide where the eye goes.

He let me stay after to help with plinths. He stood close enough to smell like oil and soap. He said, "You see edges," and I felt taller than my bones. He gave me a sketchbook. Not a gift—"a loan," he said— but I'm not dumb. It's a gift.

His eye has that crack in green. I drew it tiny in the corner of a page and wrote *sunburst*. If Cas saw she'd say boundaries like a door. I text her finish times. I keep my promises. I'm not an idiot. I am also not a child.

I'm going to get into Briarbank. I'm
going to make work that makes people shut
up.

Chapter Thirty-Two:

Worth Saving

The party winds down like a song that doesn't want to end—plates stacked, balloons half-deflated, frosting crusting on fingers. Rosaleigh melts into Charlie on the couch, two small bodies sugar-sticky, sister-shaped. It burns and it heals at once. I didn't know a heart could do both without splitting.

Sam finds me in the yard between bin bags and fairy lights. His jaw could cut thread. "You can't keep doing this, Cas. You can't keep chasing death every time you're scared to live." He doesn't need volume; it's worse in the quiet. "You have a daughter now. Two girls. Don't expect me to keep cleaning up your mess."

A shadow unhooks from the fence. Chase steps into the ring of light like he's been practicing the contours of this conversation in the dark. "And what, Sam?" His calm is a blade. "You think you're the only one who gets to save her? She doesn't need a jailer. She needs someone who sees her — who believes she's worth fighting for." He doesn't blink. "That's what I see."

The air tightens; rope pulled from both ends. Emily positions herself like a buffer; Jesse mutters a prayer without a god.

Amelia arrives like a small earthquake— stilettos sinking into lawn, perfume sharp as accusation. "Are you kidding me?" she spits, and the banner string trembles. "Her? You look at her like that? After everything I've put up with?" She flicks contempt like ash. "You'd throw me away for some broken little barmaid who can't keep herself together?"

Thanks to the night, I can feel the bruise bloom under my sleeve.

Chase doesn't look at Amelia. Not once. His eyes pin me until I can't look anywhere else. "Cas," he says, low and steady, almost pleading. "Tell me I'm wrong. Tell me you don't feel it too."

My pulse claws. Ultimatums wrestle with ghosts that still have teeth — then I see them: Charlie at the doorway, shoulders squared like a small general, Rosaleigh's fingers laced in hers so neither will drift off the edge. Both faces hold hope and fear in equal mouthfuls. They are the only jury I trust.

I spit the little stone I've been rolling with my tongue for months. "I choose them," I say. The words are granite and thin. I fold both girls in — one arm each — like my body was built to hold this particular weather. "Not your fights. Not your jealousy. Not your guilt. Them. My sister. My daughter. That's the map."

Silence lands like a verdict. Sam's fists unknot; wildfire banks to coal. Chase's shoulders fall; devastation crosses his face in a cloud. Amelia laughs — brittle and breaking — then turns it into a hiss on her way out. "You'll regret this," she throws over her shoulder, heels stabbing the dark.

I don't watch her leave. I inhale cake-sugar and Rosie's hair. Their small arms cinch. Something swivels, clicks, holds.

For a slow, clean beat, I believe it: I am worth saving.

What's left of the night creaks. Amelia's tyres shriek into the street. Emily says, "Good riddance," like a benediction with teeth. Jesse shepherds the girls inside, new instinct stamped on his face. Chase lingers long enough for guilt to look like pain; then he steps away into the shadow he's learned to drown in. "You don't understand," he tells Sam before he goes, the sentence raw. "I swore I'd keep her safe. I failed." He walks off like a practiced regret.

Sam stays a heartbeat, voice softer. "He's not wrong about some things. You are worth saving. You always were." He pauses. "But don't think the backyard makes you safe. Amelia doesn't leave. Not really. And Chase…" his helplessness tastes like ashes. "He's not done."

Later there's ice cream in a mug at the kitchen table because cold sugar makes shock obey rules. The house breathes—the fridge hum, the slow, even breathing of girls who have eaten too much cake. The yard scene loops through me. Underneath it, a treacherous truth burns steady: I didn't pick a man. I picked a life.

They expect normal at the footy-club fundraiser: meat pies, raffle books, mothers comparing thermoses. Emily drags me among the folding chairs like an anchor. Charlie is at Sam's, practicing being sister and not the small adult I keep making of her. This is what choosing looks like now: folding chairs, fairy floss, small talk with women who run canteens as if triage were a hobby.

Of course Amelia is there: arm through Chase's like a purchase with a receipt. I taste nausea and swallow it. A strip of mint gum in someone's mouth sets my stomach to boil; cucumber in the shared salad steadies it. I breathe. I hold.

"You okay?" Emily asks, eyes sharp.

"Fine," I lie, the dullest vessel.

Chase crosses later, as if he's memorised the path from his car. "Cas." His voice is small. "Didn't think I'd see you here."

"Life is full of surprises," I say. Safe words, anchors.

We talk about everything and nothing— council roadworks, the DJ's catalogue, kids who find fairy floss with unerring GPS. The current under it could drag a continent. He almost says the thing I want, and then Amelia's laugh burns through the room; he steps back like a man not ready to drown again.

"She was never yours," Emily murmurs later—two syllables that land.

"She was never mine," I answer, meaning it, hating that I do.

Wednesday: a letter slips through the mail slot. No return address, a handwriting that has no care for lines.

You can't hide forever. Nice party.

My hands shake like an actor who's forgotten a cue. I bag the paper. I don't tell Emily. I don't tell Sam. I put it in an envelope for Noor and write the time on the outside.

That night the old film reels through my skull: the door scrape, the stairs, the blade's cold in my ribs. At 2:17 I wake paralysed— the old coma's ghost pressing me flat. The music box's tune arrives late and crooked and for a half-second the knife is back as a certainty.

I fix on what saved me before: one… five… one. I count it like a spell until breath returns. When my fingers finally twitch, a sob rips out like a live wire. I drink from the tap until the cold finds my teeth. I do not wake Charlie. I do not call Chase. I fold the letter in the envelope and take it to Noor the next morning.

After hours, Take Flight opens like a small confessional. The piano is quiet, chairs overturned, the jukebox sulking. Chase lifts the lid and sets the metronome on the rail. "Two minutes," he says. Then: "We lock up, we go home."

He plays the chord we made — one… five… one — the quiet that tucks a room inward. He offers a hand, narrates his nearness because he remembers rules: "Right hand. Left shoulder." A soft, slow sway among sleeping tables. Not a kiss. Not a promise. An exchange of oxygen that doesn't hurt.

Emily walks in with a box of tea lights, face punched with blunt love. She sets the box down too gently. "Really," she says. It's not a question. "After everything? You choose this."

"It was a dance," I answer, voice small.

"It's a pattern," she replies, fierce. "Underground fights. Letters you don't tell me about. Him. I'm not your mop, Cas."

Guilt flares, ugly. "You're not my mother."

"I never tried to be." She relaxes a fraction. "I tried to be your friend. Friends say: stop feeding the thing that wants you dead." She looks to Chase, then back at me. "Choose like you mean it."

She leaves the tea lights and the quiet. The rift doesn't crack. It opens.

Chase folds his hands. "She's right," he says, almost smiling at the irony. He locks the piano. "I'll be at six a.m. if you are." Then he goes. The room remembers it's a bar.

I blow the metronome out and watch the pendulum stop.

Detective Noor — Case Notes (excerpt)

- Threat letter ("You can't hide forever. Nice party.") collected and bagged; postmark CBD; no prints (gloves likely).
- Victim reports increased sleep-paralysis and nightmares after contact with "Rowan (?)" and attendance at warehouse bouts.
- After-hours: victim + Chase slowed closeness; Emily confrontation; protective network frays. Flag: protective friend withdrawal = risk factor.
- Eyes: offender match vs. "Rowan (?)". Pull school stills near art block. Cross-check Harrow St Unit 3 tenancy.
- Amelia V.: public confrontation; influence over Eli C.; re-interview Eli re: off-site "good money" shifts.
- Next: arrange non-leading photo array incl.

Rowan (?), canvass Harrow St CCTV,

increase patrols near victim's residence.

Chapter Thirty-Four

Glass Steps

Briarbank posters bloom like algae on every tram stop between home and hospital. Charlie circles Saturdays on the calendar with a seriousness that makes me proud and sick at once.

At Rosie's bedside, she hums without noticing — a bar of Mum's old hymn turned inside out. When she concentrates, her tongue peeks from the right corner like mine did when I learned to sew. She says "Righto" the way Sam taught her and it pushes something soft sideways in me until the ache hurts less.

Emily texts logistics in emoji. When I call she doesn't pick up. Rift: present continuous.

At the gym Chase teaches footwork the way geometry can be a lifeline. We move on tape: pivot, slip, reset. He brushes my wrist by accident; we both jump like the mat burned. The look he gives — worth saving without demanding to be the rescuer — is somehow worse and better than love.

Eli arrives sober, smelling of soap and apology. "I'm off the back rooms," he says, eyes finding a horizon instead of floors. "If I ask you to hold me to that — will you?"

"Yes," I say. "But don't let yourself off easy. Ask harder."

He nods, a small, ragged victory. "Also, I got your letter to Noor out of the house before you could change your mind."

"Traitor," I say, grateful.

Saturday: I sit in the studio and become quiet made visible. Rowan critiques with a precision that flatters and commands.

"Sighting lines," he says. "Edges do the heavy

lifting. Your job is to make where to look undeniable."

Charlie laughs at something he says and the sound fills the room like heat. He glances my way once — a quick measurement — and looks away before my stare lands. When he leans close to show a rule, he narrates it: "Move the shadow, not the subject." He knows the rules that make me breathe. The speck in his eye — brown like a sunburst inside green — glints. The mark feels like a warning I don't yet have words for.

On my way home I rehearse apologies for Emily, the kind that come with tea and small bread. The words sound like me before knives.

At the flat a note is stuck under the mat in a hand that's not Emily's.

You're checking doors. Good girl.

My skin goes to ice. The harmlessness of the postal suburb collapses.

I dial Noor with my thumb shaking. She answers like a dockworker answers a bell.

"Where are you?"

"Outside," I tell her. "There's been a note. Someone's watching. Can you come?"

"I'm on my way. Don't go in."

I check our locks with hands like instruments, the same way I once checked the back bar before shift. Latch. Deadbolt. Chain. I sit outside Charlie's door until panic bleeds itself thin, counting in—four, out—until the world softens.

Later, with Rosie safe at Sam's, I turn the lounge radio low and pace to a song I don't know, counting one... five... one until the room remembers me. I am alone and steady and small and whole. Not the worst thing.

Tomorrow I will try again with Emily. Tomorrow I will tell Noor more than I want. Tomorrow I will sit in the studio chair and let my sister build a life with a man I am already watching.

That night the rabbit's ribbon is green. The blanket corners are square. The song is simple. Glass steps hold.

Detective Noor — Case Notes (excerpt)

• Note at Emily S.'s flat ("You're checking doors. Good girl.") — matched handwriting to party letter; offender surveilling victim's circle; escalate safety plan; advise route variation and lighting.

• Rowan (?) behaviour: narrates touch; precise language; may indicate grooming-style practice — keep question mark; observe for micro-grooming patterns (one-on-one invites, isolating language).

• Victim reporting mother-echo behaviours in child; psychological anchoring protective — encourage structured cues (1–5–1).

• Warehouse: temporary hiatus after party; monitor re-emergence and presence of green-eyed male.

• Immediate actions: install camera at victim's

door (done with consent), coordinate school security re: Saturday studios, request quiet patrol near Harrow St. Next interview planned with Charlie (with consent) to document Rowan's phrases ("eyes are anchors") and any odd requests.

Chapter Thirty-Five:

Lines We Don't Cross

We picnic in the hospital courtyard because the cafeteria smells like boiled beige. Sam balances a tray on one palm like a man who still thinks the world answers to courage; Rosaleigh dips carrot sticks into hummus like a tiny surgeon; Charlie steals my chips one at a time and pretends she isn't keeping score. Sun stripes the bench in neat bands. For a breath and another, the four of us fit inside a picture that doesn't pinch.

"Stop looking at me like that," Sam murmurs when the girls run to count pigeons.

"Like what?"

"Like we're a story with a neat ending." His mouth tilts. "We're not."

"I know," I say, and I don't.

At home I practice being a guardian with boundaries that don't snap. "Guardrails," I tell

Charlie. "Art club is great. The studio's great. But no after-hours one-on-ones without Ms. Patel. No locked doors. I want to meet Mr. Rowan."

Her shoulders blade. "You don't trust me."

"I don't trust rooms," I say. "Or men who make themselves into rooms."

"You don't know him." Her cheeks flare. "He sees my work. He called my eyes 'anchors' and told me to use the way people stare. He gets it."

"I get it," I say, and the truth lands soft and not at all enough. "Text me your finish time. That's the line."

"God, Cas." She laughs—mean at the edges because she's scared. "You can't fight everything."

"I can try," I say. Not the bravest answer and the only one I have.

She yanks on a hoodie and a hurt I recognise from mirrors. "Ms. Patel said I could stay late to mount work. I'm going."

"Drop a pin when you arrive."

Ten minutes pass. No pin. I text. Delivered. No read. I call Ms. Patel and hit voicemail. I call Jesse because my fight has learned to borrow better hands.

"On my way," he says before I finish.

The security light over the school gate stutters like a nervous habit. The studio is on the second floor—the windows that hold dusk longer than the rest of the building. Jesse moves ahead, shoulders turned in the way that keeps him from showing his back or his palms. The hallway smells like paint and gone-to-ink. At the end: a door, ajar. Voices.

"I can't," Charlie says, the edge of brave frayed.

"You can," a man says, soft and prying. "You'll need to if you want the scholarship panel to feel it. Hold still."

The room is staged into permissibility—lamps on, overheads off. A muslin backdrop clipped to the rail, a camera on a tripod, wine glasses sweating on a metal cart. Charlie in her jumper, rabbit ribbon looped round her wrist much too tight. Mr. Rowan behind the lens, precise, amused. He turns at our arrival and smooths his features into harmless.

"Studio practice," he says, too casual to be casual. "She's building a persona for the folio."

Jesse doesn't buy studio practice. He steps between the lens and my sister, folding muslin down so it becomes cloth instead of a set. "School policy says you don't lock doors after hours," he says mildly. "And students don't drink in rooms with staff."

"It's grape juice," Rowan answers, his smile thinner than the words.

"You're interrupting," Jesse says, and looks at Charlie, not the man. "You want to leave, kid?"

Her chin trembles. "Yes," she says, and the relief is a guilty bell. Rowan slides the camera aside with two fingers—too easy to imagine those fingers on a shoulder that isn't legal yet.

I cross the room without thinking. Chase's hand closes around my wrist midstride—iron wrapped in calm. I didn't hear

him arrive. Maybe he's been stationed in case

I remembered how to burn.

"Not like this," he murmurs. "Not in front

of her. Not so he can turn it into a scene."

"Let me go," I say, though I don't mean

it. My body presses against his steadiness the

way a struck note finds its chord. He loosens;

he doesn't leave.

Ms. Patel appears breathless and

furious—hair escaping, lanyard a bright slash.

Wine. Muslin. Man. Girl. She moves into

calm mode—the calm of someone who knows

exactly which forms to file.

"Mr. Rowan," she says, voice edged.

"Keys. Now. We'll talk in the morning with

the principal."

"It's art," he scoffs. "You can't teach fear."

"No," she says. "You can teach boundaries."

He laughs, low and wounded. "You're all cowards."

Jesse snorts. "Brother, you have no idea."

We're outside before the words have cooled. Charlie shakes in fine, furious tremors. She hates being seen like this. She shakes off my hand. "I wasn't going to do anything," she says, fierce because she's ashamed. "He just wanted—he said—"

"The rest," I say, and feel my voice go wrong. "I know." I try to keep the tone steady, practical. "I know, baby."

"Don't call me baby," she flares, then crumples into my hoodie like a child sheltering from thunder. "You embarrassed me."

"I'll be anything but sorry for showing up," I say into the heat of her hair. "I'll be sorry for not showing up fast enough."

She hiccups a laugh that isn't laughter and nods. For tonight, that counts.

Chase stands off, hands in pockets, the plane of a man who has learned not to crowd wounds. When I look up, his face is a map. I want to follow it. I want to walk away. I do neither.

"Thank you," I tell him and realize it's nowhere near enough.

"Always," he says, the word dangerous and true.

At home we make tea because ritual keeps nights from becoming caves. Charlie curls like a small animal on the couch, pencil in her hair like a talisman. "He was just going to take pictures," she murmurs. "For my folio." She swallows. "He kept saying I was special."

"You have a fifteen-year-old soul with excellent line weight," I reply. "That's enough."

She laughs brittle once. "He called me special like a debt."

We sit with it. Then she leans into me without announcing it; I pretend not to notice for exactly as long as she needs.

After Jesse leaves with promises and forms filed, after Ms. Patel texts *I'm sorry. Tomorrow 9 a.m.*, I step onto the balcony for air that doesn't smell like rooms. Sam follows. He leans against the rail.

"She ran to him," I say, hating the taste. "She ran away from me."

"She'll run back," he says. "You gave her doors. She knows which ones open to safety."

His hand brushes mine. The wild part of my heart throws a match into old tinder. We kiss—short, clumsy, and nineteen in its mistakes—and for a moment I am nineteen and stupid and not yet burned. When we pull apart I say, "We can't—"

"I know," he says. "We can want it and wait until we don't break the people who trust us."

Chase stands in the doorway with a garbage bag like a man who arrived just in time to catch the last line of a play. "Storm coming," he says, and knots the phrase like a promise.

Detective Noor — Case Notes

• School incident: studio after-hours; door ajar on arrival; set included tripod, muslin backdrop, stemware labeled "juice." Keys surrendered to HOD; Rowan suspended pending inquiry.

• Minor (Charlie): "He kept saying I was special… like it meant debt." Document exact phrasing with caution.

• Supports: Jesse H. de-escalated; Chase H. maintained perimeter; Ms. Patel initiated formal complaint.

• Action: pull school CCTV, cross-ref timeframes with Harrow St CCTV (Unit 3). Add photo array including Rowan (?) with annotation re: right-iris sunburst. Patrol near campus; arrange interview with Charlie (sensitive, trauma-informed).

Interlude — CCTV Pull (Detective Noor)

The station's footage room always smelled like old coffee and patience. Noor sat under the bank of screens, fingers a metronome on the keyboard. One monitor – schoolcam 2B, second-floor studio – crunched to life. Timestamp: Friday 19:42. Soundless, blue-tinged.

Rowan's figure appeared first: neat shoulder, satchel, practiced gait. He carried a small case—camera, maybe. He entered the studio and lingered in frame like a thumbprint. Charlie arrived at 19:46, hood up, ribbon on wrist. Rowan circled, adjusted lights. The camera's angle gave Jesse's arrival at 19:58, a body intersecting the doorway like a line through a math problem.

Noor scrubbed forward. 20:22. The set was lit differently now—lamps, low. A cart with stemware came into frame. The image blurred with motion as something else moved out of the frame, back toward the corridor. Not Jesse. A shadowed figure paused outside the studio window and then walked away down the hall.

Time check. Noor flipped to public-council cam: Harrow Street, 02:12, same week. The live feed there was grain and night. A man in a dark jacket moved across the forecourt, hood up. He paused at Unit 3, pulled a hood back, shoved something into the letterbox. Noor froze the frame and zoomed. The face was in shadow but the posture—shoulders, the way he carried himself—matched the film in the studio flicker: a neat left-handedness, the same camera case silhouette.

Noir pulled log files. Unit 3 tenancy had turned over three times in months; Amelia's name floated in the notes. The handwriting on the studio file showed Rowan as art-in-residence, on-site Fridays. She overlaid the two frames: Harrow Street 02:12; studio 19:42. Different nights, different angles. Same shape drifting in the margins of both.

She blew out a breath and ran the iris-enhancement on the best face shot she could salvage—no miracle, only a sliver of colour in one pupil. Not conclusive. But the same boots, the same left-handed reach for a prop, the same pause at thresholds. A pattern was forming like bruises along a bone.

Noor exported stills, cropped frames to show the gait and camera-bag silhouette. She annotated: *possible link Unit 3 <> Rowan (studio). Note: surveillance photo of domestic address 02:12. Recommend: covert canvas of Unit 3, interview Amelia, deep-clean of tenancy turnover. Keep Rowan under quiet observation; ask school to preserve footage; do not spook witness (Charlie).*

She sent the package to the analyst team with a note: *We're close — don't chase shadows without evidence. But watch him like he's breathing.* Then she sat very still and watched a loop of the studio for the hundredth time until the shape in the doorway stopped looking like would, could, might and more like a fact.

Corners and Bells

The amateur card was legal and bright-lit; the referee tapped the tape like an incantation. Chase wrapped my hands with the same economy as prayer. In the mirror I looked like someone meant to be in gloves. I didn't feel like it. Feeling is where you get caught.

"Corners," he said, tightening the last strip. "Find yours. Angle off. Make them miss."

"Make them pay," I muttered.

He allowed it and the permission sat with me like weight.

My opponent was compact, mean-quick. We touched gloves. Charlie—somewhere in the crowd—did commentary in a whisper: "Hands up. Breathe, idiot." The bell was a door; we stepped through.

The fight was brick-and-rubber. I made him miss air and left coins of feints on the canvas. When his punch clipped my ribs, I counted it like accounting and didn't offer interest. Between rounds Chase's voice kept me in the work: "Chin down. Step off." His words were instructions that made my body obedient.

Third round, I found one. The left hook landed where the bag had taught me force belongs. He blinked. The ref's hand rose. Decision. My name. Hands raised. For a second my bones lit like someone wired them to a substation. I wanted to vanish into the kind of violence that made me forget names.

Chase moved before the ref's hand finished. He stepped up to where the crowd parted, palms gentle on my shoulders:

"Breathe here. With me." He didn't pull me in. He let me choose gravity. I chose him.

After, alleys smelled like rain that could not decide to fall. I climbed into the truck and the world unhooked: wipers on, tyres on glass. For a moment the past leaked—Mum's laugh, headlights bloom—and I was ten and twenty and then. The seatbelt locked. My lungs did that shiver-whistle I hate. The alley tilted. A scream I didn't recognise was inside my head.

"Cas." Eli's voice was a rope. He crouched without shouting like a man who'd learned to be gentle with panic. "Five things you can see."

The grounding counted me back—sticker on the pole, shoelace, cigarette butt, a moth, my hands.

"Four you can feel." Concrete, cold, tape on my wrist, Eli's jumper.

"Three you can hear." Fridge hum, a far siren, his breathing.

"Two you can smell." Rain and lemon.

"One you can taste." Metal and mint; I hated mint.

The exercise broke the panic's teeth enough for me to laugh—grateful and small. He sat with me on the step like a brother who didn't know if he still was. "I've got you," he promised. He told a stupid joke and it worked the way a bandage works on fresh skin.

At home, the kids slept like small constellations. I stood in the doorway and let myself imagine a Sunday-life that didn't end in hospital corridors. I am reckless enough to picture markets and school notes stuck to the fridge with a green magnet and a piano in the lounge that never played a funeral.

My phone buzzed. Ms. Patel: *We've filed. He's suspended pending investigation. I'm so sorry.* Detective Noor: *Got the postcard. Patrols increased. Call me tomorrow.*

I typed the right replies, then texted Chase: *Won. Also almost broke in an alley. Eli counted me back. I'm okay.* Three dots appeared. Dissolved. Reappeared. His answer landed like a palm on my sternum: *Proud of you. Doors locked. Piano here if you need it.*

I typed *tomorrow* and didn't send the green heart.

Morning came with paperwork and interviews: Ms. Patel submitted a formal statement; Jesse took notes; Charlie sat like a soldier in case the world needed evidence.

Noor's voice over the phone was the calm you get from someone who has stitched maps of risk together before: *Save everything. Don't delete texts. Keep normal. We're covering your routes—we're watching. Don't make sudden moves.*

We tried normal. I went to clock in at the display home and pretend to show couples where afternoon light would fall. The phone hummed with the small emergencies of a life that was becoming. I checked the latch on the front door because I had a new ritual.

At dusk, washing up, a vibration on the dresser lit the screen. Unknown number.

A photo filled the display: our lounge, taken through the gap in the curtains. Charlie limp over her textbook. Rosaleigh's rabbit half-fallen. My silhouette in the doorway, head bowed.

Caption: *Corners are predictable. See you soon.*

The room stopped. The light seemed too loud. I didn't move at first. Then everything that had been in motion—Noor's CCTV frames, Ms. Patel's complaint, the studio lights, the night walks to Harrow Street— pulled together like a fist.

I reached for my phone and for the envelope already addressed to Noor. My hands didn't shake as much when I handed the screen over. Detective Noor read in a flat, efficient voice: "We've been watching him. Put that photo in evidence. Do not go home alone tonight. I'm arranging a covert patrol and a tech to pull EXIF. And—Cas—don't confront him. Not yet. We will get him."

Her *we* felt like a lifeline. But the caption's chill sat on my skin: someone had looked through curtains, had waited for the family to breathe. We were not only watched; we were timed.

I did the sensible things—changed routes, stayed at Emily's when I couldn't convince myself the house was safe, had Jesse park at odd angles so the engine would startle a watcher. I locked the door twice. I slept with my phone on the pillow and Noor's number at my thumb. But the picture sat like a fossil in my head: a camera hole, a slit in curtains, a man who'd learned to be at thresholds.

Down by the river, under corrugated roofs and fluorescent bloom, the underground fights rearranged their rules. Prize money rose, referees tightened rules, and the crowd got hungrier—danger now a commodity. The green-eyed men that people noticed in the back rows looked like a pattern. A face in the crowd, a gait in barley-light, a note clenched between teeth.

At home, with a child's rabbit in my lap and three surveillance screenshots saved to a secure folder, I pressed my palm to the old X on my chest and counted: one… five… one. Breathe until the room remembered the shape of me. Then I sent the photo to Noor, the shot that had come to my phone, the caption included.

Her reply was almost instant: *We have a line. Don't be alone. Wait for my team. He'll make a mistake.*

The last light outside the curtains went out like an eyelid. The house felt watched, which meant we could no longer pretend we weren't.

Detective Noor — Case Notes (urgent)

• Amateur bout: victim present; won by decision; post-event photo surveillance. Eli C. effective grounder.

• School action: Rowan suspended; statements scheduled. Preserve all footage. Interview HOD re: keys.

• Fresh escalation: surveillance photo of victim's lounge sent to her phone (caption: "Corners are predictable. See you soon."). EXIF request sent; forensic team assigned.

• Immediate actions: covert patrol on victim residence; increase school patrols; canvass Harrow St for doorbell or porch camera footage; request tenancy turnover records for Unit 3.

• Threat assessment: offender comfortable surveilling domestic spaces; proximity increased; urgency = HIGH. Keep victim insulated from direct confrontation; goal = identify > arrest.

Officer on the

The letter arrives folded like a threat that knows origami: *You're not untouchable.*

We bag it. We log it. We breathe in a way that's a fraction slower than panic.

The detective who meets us at the station is new to our file but not new to this work. Her badge reads NOOR. Her voice makes fear pick a seat.

"Detective Noor," she says, palms open and steady. "I'll be lead." She takes the evidence sleeve without small talk and reads the handwriting like a fingerprint. "Same loop on the y," she notes. "Same ink weight. Careful. That's useful."

Her phone buzzes; she silences it without apology. "I'll be in touch. Often," she promises.

Outside, the air presses down with false heat. Charlie thumbs a message so fast the screen blurs. "Studio," she says, already angling away. "Ms. Patel said I can finish before the show."

"Daylight only," I say. "Doors open. Pin me your location when you get there."

She salutes with two fingers and a half-grin, then the hallway takes back its sound. The kitchen clock gets loud.

"Noor — Then."

Rain chewed the road in sheets the day the call came. Noor had been on the bonnet of her car, half-curdling a coffee that tasted like burnt apologies, when the dispatcher clipped the words: two-car, rural, possible entrapment. She pointed the ute at the dark and drove like someone bargaining with the weather.

The truck's nose had been buried in wire and dirt; tyre tracks scribbled at the verge. Petrol hissed from the ditch. A tall girl in wet denim stood in the rain with blood on her mouth, one arm wrapped around a smaller body she'd already pulled free.

"Constable Noor," the teenager had said, voice too steady. "My parents won't wake up."

Noor peeled off her jacket and wrapped both girls, shoulder to shoulder. Keep the small one looking at you. Keep the big one counting. She remembers the way the tall girl counted under her breath—four in, six out—until the small one's sob hiccuped into air. Holding the living until they remember how to stand: sometimes the job is that simple and that impossible.

—Now.

The art-block corridor smells of turps and finishing spray. Jesse rounds the corner into a quiet that looks chosen. A door sits ajar—lamp-light, not fluorescents; a muslin backdrop clipped to a rail; a tripod waiting like a polite accusation. Two glasses sweat on a metal trolley.

"School policy: no locked rooms after hours," Jesse says. He steps into the light like gravity has no argument.

"It's a still life," Rowan says, professional warmth folded to a practiced smile. "Everyone's safe."

Charlie stands under the lamp like a small sun. Ribbon at her wrist, chin high. "I'm fine," she says too fast.

The light swings when Rowan turns. Green, bottle-glass green—brown sunburst in the right iris, like a fossilised lightning strip. The memory digs in; a scar in the dark wakes clean and sharp.

My feet move before my head catches up. Chase's palm finds my wrist and steadies, not holding, just lending weight. "Not like this," he says, low. "Not in front of her."

Ms. Patel arrives furious with paperwork on her tongue. She goes calm in the way people who know forms do—precise and clinical. "Keys," she says, palm up.

Rowan's smile thins. "Art requires risk," he says.

"Boundaries are not optional," Ms. Patel replies. The keys slide into her hand, metallic and final.

We're in the corridor before any of us knows we're moving. Charlie catches my sleeve—small fingers that've been a human compass—and whispers, "I wasn't going to." The relief is a lurch I swallow.

Jesse files the report. Chase puts distance between the man and the exit without fuss. Ms. Patel texts the principal and finally breathes.

Later, in our kitchen, Noor sits like a map you can read. She slides a card across to me. "Two matters: the letters and the school." Her gaze lands on Charlie and softens with the kind of authority that has both hands full of grief and a badge.

"You were good at leaving records that hold," she says, and it is both a compliment and a charge.

"Have we met?" Charlie asks.

Noor holds off the past. "A long time ago. Different job," she says. It's the kind of truth that tilts toward mercy.

She leaves numbers, instructions, and a presence that takes the edge off the room. On her way out she pauses at the crooked tree. The silver bauble throws our faces back, bent and bright. "Good," she says into the yard, and in that small way means the whole house.

That night Chase places a card in my hand: Amateur bout—Jan 12. "Sanctioned," he says. "If you need the bell, take the bell."

"I don't need—" I start.

He looks at me like a man who knows myself better than I do. I lace my shoes.

Between rounds, his temple finds mine—sweat, salt, nothing polite left. "You keep living," he says. "Even when it's ugly."

"I'm getting greedy for it," I answer, and the smile we share is a private contract.

On the tram home my phone buzzes: unknown—*Nice keys. Shame about the doors.* I forward it to Noor before my hands learn to shake.

Detective Noor — Case Notes

- New letter: same "y" loop, consistent ink pressure.

- After-hours studio: Rowan relinquished keys; HOD present; union to meeting.

- Patrol directive: evening pass-by at residence + school; install doorbell cam.

- Suspect: **Rowan (?)** Iris anomaly (R eye "sunburst"); cross-ref w/ Harrow St Unit 3.

- Victim safety: assign uniform "on the door" presence evenings for 1 wk.; vary routes.

- Note: Caregiver fatigue in Emily— monitor support network tension (can fracture safety plan).

Chapter Thirty-Nine:

Edge

The underground bouts had rules the legal scene liked—sanctioned, refereed, IDs checked—but you still left a bit of your soul in the floor. People came to watch other people stop thinking with their problems and start thinking with their fists. It was pragmatic theatre.

I told myself the sanctioned match was cleaner. I told myself I would box like a practitioner and not a terrified animal. I told myself a lot of things until the night unpeeled them.

The alley stank of river damp. Neon haloed pallets. I wrapped my hands slow because Chase's fingers moved with prayer. "Corners," he said, like a benediction. "Own them. Angle off. Don't chase the hit."

The bell cracked the air and we began. I moved like I had taught myself to move—jab, cross, step. Memory and violence matched cadence. The crowd's roar plugged a hole in my chest and for three rounds it was almost clean. Then the man from the back row—the one who laughed too sharp when I stepped into range—pushed his way forward. He shouldn't have been where he was, not after alert. He smelled of river and old beer and something like ammonia. He kept returning to the ring edge like a cadaver recalled.

After my limit, I left the ring dizzy with adrenaline and laughter, at once fierce and brittle. He followed me out.

"You fight like a woman," he said, slurring that nothing in the modern world makes less sense than the leftover privileges of commentary.

"Maybe you should stop watching," I told him.

He grinned with too many teeth and shoved into my space. The shove was small, the kind that says *this is my wont*. I stepped back.

It turned into a shove-and-step. A flash of hands where his aim is to humiliate and to startle and my body, I think, remembered the wrong room and the wrong stitches and chose.

I hit him. It wasn't careful. It wasn't pretty. I meant to stop him from being a danger to anyone else. My left hook caught jaw, his mouth opened, blood made a tally across his lip. He stumbled and then reached for a bottle—someone's beer. The smell of it made me see another man years ago, hood up, blade catching light.

He lunged. I blocked because lessons are muscle memory. He went for my throat with a fury I hadn't seen outside places that sell fear. The world narrowed to a face and a blade of intention.

I didn't know I had that kill-breed inside me until I did. The instinct is not noble; it's a blade with a name you learned when you were made to be small. My fist moved to stop him the way a surgeon's hand goes to an incision—precise, too hard, relentless.

He fell to the ground hard. The circle surged and two hands—Sam's, then Chase's—tore me off like yanking a live wire from a socket. I was panting and not because of the gloves. My knuckles were sharp where skin had split on stubborn teeth. My breath tasted of iron.

Chase put both hands on my shoulders as if to check if the spine inside was still mine. Sam's face had lost its colour. For a second the two of them were not only friends and supports but witnesses to an edge I had walked around for years and now exposed like a bone.

"You nearly killed him," Chase said later, voice that was more a fact than accusation. "Do you know that?"

I couldn't feel the question because I was too far out on the flat. "He had a knife," I said. "He'd already pushed me. He—"

"He had a bottle," Sam interrupted, the type of correction that refuses to let you make a martyr of monsters. "We saw the bottle. He was on his feet. He was more than drunk."

Noor arrived minutes later because Noor is tuned to the vector of escalation. She came with an ambulance crew and a patrol car and a steady voice that leeched adrenaline of drama.

"I need statements," she said, practical as a scalpel. "Everyone who was near the ring. A witness log. Hospital for the man—head split. You, Cass, are volatile right now. We'll take your statement when you are coherent."

They took the man away on a stretcher; he spat and cursed in the back of the van. His eyes were not amber; they were ordinary river-eyed and frightened. He said my name as if it was a thing thrown at him. Some of the crowd claimed they saw him watching me for weeks; others said he'd only been in town a month. Noor took them seriously anyway.

At the station later, when the initial tide of people was done and Sam and Chase's hands finally released me, Noor sat across from me and asked, with the gentlest authority, *Did you mean to hurt him like that?*

I thought of the nights with the sound of knives; I thought of the way my ribs had been an X of a map to hold someone back; I thought of the quiet in my bone that had been tempered into anger that doesn't weep. "I meant to finish the scare," I said. "I meant to make him stop following me. I didn't mean—" My voice breaks on the simple grammar.

Noor's eyes didn't blink in a judgement I could read. "We have to understand escalation," she said. "But I will also tell you something, and it's not a permission slip: you are human, Cass. Not a weapon. Not hollow. The thing they made you into does not have to be your forever."

Chase's face had folded a dozen ways by then. He'd seen that same lastness once before. Later, in the quiet of the carpark as we walked back, he told Sam a part of his history he'd said in fewer words to others—a memory of getting broken and being fixed.

He'd been discharged from the army— worse than tired and poorer than he expected—and his left leg had been a constellation of pain. He'd stumbled out of the hospital into the wrong part of town and into a bar that had no reason to be kind. A kid— Eli—had seen him sitting in a corner like garbage and had offered the last clean napkin and a beer and a hand up. Eli had been small and awkward and steady; he'd sat and bandaged Chase's leg with a strip of T-shirt until they could get proper help. Chase had thought, then, that someone like Eli was luck and nothing more. Now he looked at Eli and saw the human who had borrowed a coat and a patch and not pressed for anything in return.

"Eli saved me a stupid way," Chase said. "He kept me from falling into that hole that swallows good men who don't get a hand up. He just… stayed." He stopped, a flash of gratitude, and looked at me with an intensity that was part apology for having needed help and part vow that he would be the help for me.

It changed how I saw Eli—no longer a bartender with shaky choices but a man who had once held a stranger's leg together and not used it as currency. It explained the steadiness under his jokes, the way his counting had steadied me in an alley. It was the small human story used to stitch a bigger, stranger narrative.

After the fight the legal work began slow and precise. Statements. Witness forms. Forensics took a swab of the man's clothing and ran the camera footage again. Noor spoke quietly with me at the back of the station: "You were right to show up. We needed witnesses. We needed a scene. But we need you alive for the long work ahead."

I stared at my hands, raw and knuckled, and listened to the policing of my own life. The man's assailant breath rattled in a cell; whether it would be assault charges or

misadventure folded into the court's calculus
was beyond my immediate control. The police
argument and the hospital reports would
resolve one way or another.

What I felt physically, most of all, was
numb—like a limb reclaimed after frost. The
anger had served me; its job was to save. But
now it sat like a used tool: it had done the
saving; it wanted to be set down.

Sam and Chase had seen the side of me
that doesn't ask for permission, and the sight
of it changed them. Chase's jaw was stone the
whole way home. Sam's hands trembled when
he poured tea. Both men had the same look in
their faces: the true, awful recognition that the
person they loved could become lethal and
justify it.

Noor's voice in my ear later was both tender and professional. "We'll push hard on Harrow St. We'll keep the photo trail open. We'll bring your support—no lone walks. And—Cass—if this edge wants to stay, we will get you trained to keep the law on the right side. But try to let the team be the violence when it needs to be. You owe the girls you keep one alive mother."

I let the words sink in with the weight of the night. I wanted to be both guardian and avenger; I had to learn when the balance would tip.

When I lay in bed that night, my knuckles bandaged, Chase's old jacket across the foot, I counted like a ritual: one… five… one. The number steadied me in the same way Noor's forensics would steady the case. The net was tightening, and someone was watching. The watchman had misread corners as predictability. He was wrong.

We were not untouchable — and now we were deciding who would be allowed to touch us at all.

Chapter Forty:

Who Needs Superheroes When You Have a Sister

It happens on an ordinary Thursday that doesn't know it's important. The sky is the particular grey that makes school uniforms look bluer. Charlie hums while she makes lunch like she's auditioning for a kitchen musical, peanut-butter stripe on her cheekbone like war paint. Rosaleigh sits on the bench, rabbit under her arm, eyes narrowed with the seriousness small children bring to the process of watching older girls be older girls.

Somewhere between the clink of the knife in the sink and Charlie licking a smear off her thumb, I notice—the ache that used to live between my ribs like a lodger has moved out. Not forever. Not for always. But the weight has shifted. What's in its place feels like certainty with dirty sneakers.

We walk to school because the tram is a story we don't owe the day. Charlie skips the bit where you're supposed to be too cool to skip. She calls out to friends and is called back by name, not by eyes. Rosaleigh tugs my hand for courage and curiosity. Watching them, something unclenches low in my belly. We are not fine. We are okay. Okay is a country you can choose to live in.

Charlie comes home with a jumper that looks like it lost a fight with concrete and knees that confirm it. "They said I needed saving," she mutters, trying to be casual and failing. "Like I can't take care of myself."

I kneel so our faces level. "You don't need saving," I say, brushing gravel out of palm lines like reading, "but you've got me anyway."

Her mouth does the stubborn thing; her eyes do the teary one. "Like a superhero?"

I laugh because the word in her mouth is too big and just right. "Better. Superheroes fly away when the credits roll. Sisters do the dishes."

She searches me for loopholes. Doubt gives way like a wave that finally decides to be shore. "Even when I'm annoying?"

"Especially then."

She smirks with the dignity of a queen who knows her court will tolerate exactly this much insolence. That night, a ridiculous cape from a Halloween box we never returned reappears. Rosaleigh crawls under the blanket with us, eyes huge, and Charlie throws an arm over her like a training montage. "See?" she tells her, as if this were always obvious. "Now I get to be your superhero too."

Rosaleigh giggles in the small way that makes you put a hand on your heart like you forgot it was there. It's the first laugh in weeks that didn't feel coaxed. I kiss both heads because it's a habit we earned, not a reflex.

We keep the TV on too loud and let a caped idiot solve problems by punching robots because the world is heavy and metaphor is a mercy. When the credits roll, the girls boo the end because they want the happy to keep happening. And I realise I've been waiting for rescue so long I missed the obvious: we've been rescuing each other in increments—toast made without asking, hands held, art hung on fridges, the way

Charlie says always when she doesn't mean later.

Saturday, we take wildflowers to the cemetery because visiting is a promise, not a superstition. Eucalyptus throws its clean knife into the air. Headstones sit like people at a bus stop trying to remember route numbers. Charlie kneels and arranges stems with surgical solemnity. She brushes leaves from Mum and Dad's names like she's waking them gently.

"Do you think they can see us?" she asks, not looking at me, as if the words would go brittle if we looked straight at them.

"I like to think they can," I say. "And that they're proud of how loud we keep getting up."

"It still hurts," she says.

"It always will." The honesty sits between us like an adult with good posture. "Love doesn't leave when people do. It changes address."

Rosaleigh's voice threads in. "So… they're still with us?"

"Always," I say, tucking hair behind her ear because that is also always.

On the way to the car, Rosaleigh takes my left hand and Charlie takes my right. A triangle of warmth in a morning that chews fingers. We are not a tidy family. We are the kind you assemble. The ache remains. So does the love. That's the whole trick.

At home, the mailbox coughs up two envelopes: one from council thick enough to be good news, one thin white liar. We open hope first. The letter offers me the council role—probationary months attached like training wheels. We scream in the kind way and spin in the kitchen until dizziness makes its case.

Only then do I open the thin one. *See you soon, angel.* No envelope, no stamp. Hand-delivered. Charlie clocks my face and her shoulders pull themselves wider.

"We tell the detective," she says. No question mark. We bag it. We log it. We send the photo. We move the kitchen chair under the back door because ritual has teeth.

Eli swings by with groceries I didn't ask for—bread, cucumbers, the good peanut butter—eyes clear, hands steady. He notices the cape taped to the wall, the skyline we've drawn underneath.

"Headquarters," he reads. "Sisters Incorporated."

"You can be Night Shift," Charlie decides, awarding him a sticky-note badge. He laughs, a little wrecked, and for once I don't hear alcohol in the edges. Only effort.

When people ask for the shape of our days, I don't know how to give it without handing them the whole blueprint—the alarms and the art, the drills and the dancing; Chase at six a.m. with mitts and patience; Jesse on the back steps with unvarnished confession; Emily with lists and love like a scolding; Sam showing up with a spare car seat he didn't ask permission to buy; Eli trying and failing and trying again in the quiet you only see if you stop judging; Amelia circling like weather I refuse to be surprised by.

We're not saved by capes. We're not doomed by cracks. We are made by the hands we hold and the doors we lock and the mornings we get up and the nights we sit on cold steps until the heat leaves the concrete.

Superheroes leave when the city is quiet. Sisters stay for dishes, fundraising forms, midnight fevers, meetings with people who say probationary and mean we'll see, and letters you plastic-sleeve so your fear has a filing system.

Some nights Sam falls asleep in the visitor chair with frosting on his cuff from a cupcake someone handed him because he looked like a dad. Some mornings Chase's piano lamp is still on when I arrive—one stool, two cups—*Glass Wings* waiting in the quiet. I stand between them like a person at a fork in a road. Family I lost and found. Future I could earn. I don't choose. Not today. Today I count one… five… one and keep the doors locked.

We're not waiting for rescue anymore. We're building the city.

Charlie's POV: Field Notes on Capes

People think capes mean flight. They mostly mean tripping hazards and a dramatic exit.

Cas says sisters do the dishes and I believe her, even when I'm wearing the cape and she's burning the toast. (She says "caramelized," which is a lie with sugar.)

At school they said I needed saving. I wanted to say: I have a sister; that's better. I didn't. I pushed back with my mouth first because fists make paperwork and Ms. Patel says line weight solves more than you think.

Rosie asked if Mum and Dad could still see us. I said yes before Cas could, which felt like telling the sky how to weather. Then I drew their names on the fogged car window and she didn't tell me to stop. She took a picture. She's learning.

Mr. Rowan taught me how to sight lines. Jesse taught me how to sight exits. Cas taught me how to count. Chase taught me how to keep my hands up. Eli taught me that coming back is a skill. Emily taught me that lists are spells. Sam taught me how to cut cucumbers the way kids will actually eat them. Amelia taught me to keep the cape out of open flames.

Field note: I don't need saving; I need witnesses who don't blink.

When I can't sleep, I wear the cape and do the dishes. It is impossible to be entirely sad while wearing a cape and scrubbing spaghetti sauce. Science.

.

Whispers

Avalanches start with a whisper.

Emily's barbs come as half-jokes that don't land. "Some of us have partners to go home to," she says when Jesse lingers on the steps with soup and a wrench.

We argue. We apologise. We argue again. Later she stands in my lounge with her arms crossed like she's holding herself together.

"Everyone sees it," she says. "The way he looks at you." Her mouth trembles. "Where does that leave me?"

"You're my sister," I say. "I don't want him, Em. I never have."

Truth lands and still the room keeps the echo.

Hell's Gates—warehouse heat, copper air. A taped square pretending to be rules. First bout: bruised pride I can afford. Second:

education I can't. Then he's there—green-bottle eyes with the hairline brown lightning I tried to file into myth. The room narrows to a corridor with a door I know too well.

He moves like a nightmare that wrote the choreography. The knife becomes a fist. The stair becomes a heel. I go down. His smile is the same. The floor rises to meet me like old carpet.

In the car park, the air tastes like oil and panic. Sam is a furnace to my left; Chase is a cut-glass prayer to my right.

"It was him," I rasp. "The man who—" The sentence is a room I can't walk into.

Chase cups the back of my neck like he's bringing me up from deep water. Our foreheads touch. "You're not alone," he says, voice a thread. "Not this time."

The choice sparks like tinder. Sam clears his throat and the world remembers itself.

But that's not the whole night.

Later—because adrenaline is a currency that buys bad decisions—I hear there's a sanctioned undercard two blocks over. The taped square is cleaner, the refs official; the place smells better and worse at once. I go because the itch is loud and because sanctioned means rules and because sometimes rules are all the theatre left to us.

My opponent is a man with calm shoulders and hands that have been paid to hurt. He comes at me fast; I come at him faster. Punches are paragraphs we read aloud—short, staccato, making meaning. He falls into the rhythm I built with Chase: hands up, breathe, step. The ref shouts and counts like they invented mercy.

Then a cheap thing happens—an elbow, illegal, clipped across my jaw. Blood hot and immediate. I turn with the animal I kept alive; something in me slides the safety off. I land a blow that makes his face fold in a way that could be the end of him. The whole room freezes—sudden saint and jury at once.

I stand over him. My gloves smell like iron and regret. There's a teatime moment when the simple physics of a punch becomes a moral ledger. Every second stretches greedy. The man isn't moving. His mouth parts like someone searching for a prayer.

Chase's shout cuts the still. Sam's hands are inside my shoulders before I can think.

"Cas—stop!" he says. Not pleading.

Command. The voice I've been repelling inwardly for months anchors me by muscle and memory.

I want to finish it. I want to make the world understand how close I came to losing everything. I want to press the button and be done. But then I see Chase's face at the edge of the ring—the same face from the night the X happened, the same haunted patience—and I don't. I step back as tears and sweat and blood rain down. The ref calls time. Hands pull me into the corridor like I'm a body no one wants to admit to loving too much.

Sam and Chase look at me with a new kind of careful. Pride and fear live in the same pair of eyes. For a long terrible flash I am the person who can finish things. For an even longer one, I am the person who didn't.

That night, the car park smells like everything we can't fix. Eli is there. He was the one who taught Chase to count breath again years ago, after a different kind of fight. (They met when Chase was coming home on discharge and a drunk driver had folded his leg like paper; Eli — then a volunteer in a hospital kitchen — had found him under rubble and ferried him in blankets to an ambulance. Eli's hands still remember how to hold bone steady. Chase owes him his footing.) Eli slides into the space without drama and counts with me until my head unknots.

"No more basements," Charlie had told me. Jesse told Emily. Emily told her. Promises sit light until they have to be heavy. Splinters collect in the soft places.

Morning cracks open and Emily bursts in with an apology that shakes. "I was wrong," she says, eyes too bright. "I'm late."

The word detonates and remakes the air. Pregnant.

Joy arrives like a stray that decides to stay. Jesse appears in the doorway as if he rehearsed the timing, his hand finding hers like he never lost it. We let the future out of its box and let it run laps around the kitchen. Charlie squeals; the neighbour's dog volunteers harmonies. For one ridiculous afternoon, hope has elbows.

That night I go to the storm-water pit— the city's forgotten pupil—because I need a bigger room for the noise in my head. Chase is already on the rail, hands in pockets, looking like a man who learned to breathe here first.

We sit with our shoulders almost touching and count—four in, four hold, six out—until the city lines up with itself. The dark carries our breath back like tide.

"Sometimes I think I'm bad luck," I say. "Like I walk into rooms and the floor starts doing maths."

"Sometimes I think I'm a hammer and everything's a nail," he says. "We're both wrong. But even if we're not, hammers are useful and luck is just a story."

"Tell me something good."

He does. The DJ who wore a cardigan sent a playlist called *Glass Wings*. Jesse cried when Emily showed him the second line on the test. Eli did a meeting, white-knuckled and sober. Sam bought the world's ugliest second-hand car seat and cried in Bunnings when no one was looking. The girls fell asleep head-to-head under the cape taped to the wall.

I lean that last inch and rest my head under his jaw. It is not a kiss and it is not, not a kiss.

"If we do this," I say, "we do it slow."

He grins into my hair. "Geologic time."

We count again. Four in. Four hold. Six out.

On the last out, my breath catches. Two lights float in the pit's water—green as old glass, unwavering. For a second they look like eyes.

"What?" he asks.

"Nothing," I lie, and force the air the rest of the way. He doesn't push. We jump down from the rail like people who trust their knees

and start back toward the lights of the main

road.

Two blocks from Take Flight, a thin lick

of smoke finds us—sharp, chemical, wrong.

We look at each other once and run.

Chapter Forty-Two:

Carols in a Key We

Know

By late afternoon the flat smells like cinnamon and sunscreen and people. The tree leans like it's listening. Jesse squeezes a narrow upright through the doorway with a noise usually reserved for childbirth and furniture removalists. Three keys stick, two are heroic, the finish is scuffed to honesty.

"Gumtree miracle," he pants. "Tuned enough to pass a breath test."

Chase runs a hand along the wood like he's apologising for the city. He sits. The first chord lands warm and a little crooked. It sounds exactly like us.

Emily strings the last run of popcorn and pretends not to look at Jesse's hands as he wipes his brow with the hem of his T-shirt. Sam arrives with pavlova pretending to be a cloud and a wrapped shoebox for Rosaleigh

that is very obviously not shoes. Charlie
positions herself where she can supervise
everything at once and be supervised by no
one.

"Requests?" Chase asks, flexing fingers. I
slide onto the bench beside him, hip to hip,
like we have always known how to share a
small space.

"Something not about snow," I say. "The
only white we're getting is icing sugar."

He smiles sideways. "Deal."

He finds a key that isn't sticky and rolls
into a tune that wants to be a carol without
lying about it. I hum first, then sing—low, not
brave yet. Emily's harmony threads in like a
dare. Jesse taps rhythm with two fingers on
the lid. Charlie laughs; Rosaleigh, newly
emboldened by the shoebox, joins on the same

syllable every line with the commitment of a choirgirl who hasn't learned doubt.

Between verses, he shifts to something small and green at the edges.

"What's that?" I ask.

"Play it once and I'll tell you," he says, nodding for me to try. The melody fits in my mouth better than most nights do. It feels like remembering a road you've never driven. When we finish, he whispers, "We can call it Emerald. You make it glow."

The room goes gently quiet around that.

Presents are chaos. Rosaleigh opens the shoebox and gasps at the rabbit-sized wardrobe inside—tiny ribboned collars, one emerald, one sky. Sam pretends he didn't stay up two nights stitching badly and I pretend I don't see the needle pricks.

We eat on our laps because plates are a theory. We sing again because the first time didn't break the room. Chase leans in, shoulder to mine; every shared note tightens a string I've been plucking for months. When I catch Emily watching from the kitchen with a look I can't read, I overcorrect—louder, safer—and miss a chord. Chase covers for me without making a hero of it.

Later, baths and bedtime. Charlie volunteers to rinse conditioner from small curls like she invented the technique. I dry while Sam reads the rabbit wardrobe a bedtime story as if integrity requires it. When Rosaleigh's eyes start doing the slow-blink of surrender, I sit on the edge of her mattress and talk about Mum and Dad because I promised myself I would tell our history out loud where it can't fester.

"Mum cut sandwiches into triangles," I say, smoothing hair the way she always forgave it. "She swore they tasted braver that way."

"Grandad wore a hat even to the letterbox," Charlie adds from the doorway, soft. "He said magpies respected a man with a brim."

"They sang badly," I say, and Chase's chuckle from the hall makes my throat do a thing I blame on dust. "But they sang."

"Are they here?" Rosaleigh asks, not scared—curious.

"In the stories," I say. "In the way we laugh. In the way we don't give up."

She nods like a judge ruling in our favour, then slides instantly into sleep, mouth open, rabbit wedged like a witness.

We drift back to the lounge where the tree hums. Emily stacks plates harder than necessary. Jesse tries to kiss the back of her neck and lands on shoulder blade because she moves. He retreats to bin bags. The dent in the room holds.

Sam ducks to the car and returns with a cracked leather album. "Found this," he says, offering it like contraband.

Farm sky. Ute, perfect and terrible. My mother twenty-three and invincible in a dress that had no right to be worn in dirt. My father with grease under his nails and pride in his eyes. Me and Sam under floodlights at the fair, his palm sticky with fairy floss, my grin all trouble. I laugh in a key I don't use anymore; it hurts and helps.

We turn pages slower than time. He leans in to point—there, the dam; there, the kitchen radio; there, your hair the colour of bad ideas—and suddenly we are too close and exactly right. His thumb ghosts my jaw to wipe a happy tear; the album slides to my lap; the kiss is a question we both answer without words.

At sixteen we were tinder—fairground floodlights and cheap speakers, all heat, no handrails. We burned in circles, fast and foolish, swore we'd never stand near that fire again. And here it is, years later, banking itself into something steadier, testing if heat can be a hearth and not a warning.

It tastes like sugar and apology and the years we didn't get. It is soft, then not. My hand finds his shirt like it remembers the map. Heat climbs my spine and every choice I've postponed lines up outside the door and bangs to be let in.

"Cas?" Chase's voice from the hall—two letters full of stepping back. He stops just inside the doorway and sees the room the way it is, not the way anyone meant it to be.

We break like light through leaves. I sit up too fast; the album thumps shut.

"It's not—" I start, which is never a sentence that ends well.

Chase tries to smile and fails with dignity. "Looks like exactly what it is," he says, careful. "I'll… head out."

"Chase—" I find my feet; the room tilts half a notch.

He sets the shortbread tin on the bench like an offering he can't take back. "Merry Christmas," he says, and the way he looks at me hurts in places I thought were scar.

After the door clicks, the apartment exhales like it's been holding in different weather. Emily emerges and clocks the plates: me wrecked, Sam wrecked, a ghost of a melody still working the air.

"I knew it," she says, not triumph—tired. She doesn't meet Jesse's eyes when he reappears with bags. He doesn't ask. The gap between them is a canyon lit by fairy lights.

When the house finally sleeps, I sit under the tree with the album open to my parents kissing like they meant it. Joy and regret braid. My chest is a bruise made of choices; I press a palm to it and promise neither man anything. I promise the girls everything. Then I blow out the scented candle and the day.

Outside, somewhere, a match is struck. We don't smell it yet.

Chapter Forty-Three:

Ember Lines

Morning is a fog of pancake batter and the taste of things unsaid. Charlie studies me over the whisk like she's checking a compass. Sam makes Dad's bad coffee on purpose and we laugh like we didn't ruin the map. Jesse takes a call on the balcony that turns his shoulders to granite; Emily rinses a mug until the glaze should wear off.

Text from Officer Noor at 9:12: Small bin fire behind your block at 3 a.m. Extinguished fast. Likely lit. Patrols increased. Cameras requested. You, okay?

We're okay, I type, which is both report and defiance.

At lunch the girls nap in a tangle that rewrites my DNA. Two messages wait like coins: *Can we talk?* from Chase. We shouldn't, but I can't pretend last night didn't happen from Sam. I set the phone face-down and go learn the choreography for not breaking in public.

The crack with Charlie starts small—a wince when I suggest a tram together, a sigh when I remind her to pin her location, a quiet *I've got it* with sharp edges when I check the back door twice.

"I'm not prey," she snaps when I hover in her doorway. "I don't want to live in your fear."

"It's not mine," I say, too calm to be believed. "It's ours."

"That's worse," she fires back. "Yours got loud. Mine didn't get a chance."

Welts bloom on words. "This is about Rowan," I say, and the name changes the room's shape.

"He's suspended," she says, defensive. "He's opening a pop-up over summer. Community classes. He sees me."

"He targeted you," I say, one inch from a shout. "That's not seeing. That's scouting."

Her jaw sets. "You don't get to be the only person in this house who wants to be wanted."

Silence is the right answer; I miss it. "You didn't see his eyes," I say. "I did."

She flinches at the unfair part, grabs her bag like momentum can outrun shame, and leaves a door click behind.

I text Ms. Patel and Jesse, then Noor— care is a net, not a solo. Replies stack fast:

Ms. Patel: Pop-up flyer attached. He's listed. We're on it.

Jesse: Passing that block anyway.

Noor: Do not engage alone. I'll brief uniform.

The block Rowan rented smells like fresh paint and cheap intent. Windows taped with butcher paper. A sandwich board with his name that doesn't mention the school. I stand across the street and breathe through the urge to light it on administrative fire.

"Don't," Jesse says, arriving with a shadow broader than a man should own. "She texted. She's at the library."

Relief drops me a foot; anger fills the space. "Holiday timing," I say. "Fewer guards, more kids."

"Different gatekeepers," he says, eyes on doors, angles, blind corners. "We'll be them."

Back home, Rosaleigh nestles into my lap with the photo album and points at Mum's hands in every picture. "She's always fixing," she says, proud.

"We all are," I answer, kissing the top of her head. "It runs in the family."

At dusk, the bin behind our block wears caution tape like a joke. Eli leans against it with the defensive humour of a man who'd rather be the punchline than the problem. "Wasn't me," he says, hands up.

"I know," I say, and mean it.

We stand in the alley until the light goes copper. The wrong footstep in the wrong place flicks every switch I own. Panic rises like tide; my knees choose the old story. Eli reads the angle and shifts without touching.

"Okay," he says. "Inventory." He walks me through the world like it's a room we can open windows in. When my breath lands again, I lean my head against cool brick and let his shoulder hold the rest.

"You don't have to be the bravest at every fire," he says.

"I don't know how not to be."

"Then let me be brave at the boring ones," he says. "Bins, locks, escorting you to the letterbox like a Victorian aunt."

I snort-laugh, which means I'm alive.

At ten, the phone orbits the truth again. I answer Chase first because the room in my chest with his name on it needs airing.

He's outside with the shortbread tin I wouldn't let him take home. "I'm not here to ask," he says. "I'm here to say I'm not going anywhere. You chose the girls. Good. I wanted to be the person you chose, too. But I can live being the man who helps you stay alive."

"That's a lot to give."

"It's not give," he says. "It's keep." He taps the tin. "Emerald's still yours, whenever you want it."

After he goes, I call Sam. We don't touch the kiss first. We talk about a seven-year-old who wrote *MUM* twice on the same drawing because the first one looked lonely, about vaccines, about whether rabbits can eat kale. At the end, soft: "If there's a world where we try again, I want it," he says. "But I won't be the reason you can't breathe."

"I'm already breathing," I say, which is confession and miracle. "I just don't know which way to walk."

"Then I'll stand here," he says, and means a driveway, a ward, a year.

The flat is a dark aquarium, fairy lights blinking like patient fish. Charlie's door opens and pauses the way it used to when she didn't yet know doors can keep you safe and alone.

"You awake?" she asks.

"Always," I answer, a word I owe carefully.

She folds onto the couch, knees to chin, fortress lowered. "Ms. Patel sent the school-wide email," she says. "He's suspended. There's a meeting. Noor asked for my statement."

"I know," I say. "I'm sorry I made you feel like you had to choose between being seen and being safe."

She nods, small. "I hate that we have to pick."

"We don't," I say, trying the truth I'm still learning. "We can make rooms where both fit."

She rests her head on my shoulder like muscle memory. "You kissed Sam," she says. Not a question.

"I did," I say. "And I told Chase he mattered. Neither answer solves tonight."

"Grown-ups are ridiculous," she says—fair. "But… the song was pretty."

"Emerald," I say.

"Figures." She rolls her mismatched eyes. "You'd name a thing after a colour."

We sit with the not-knowing on purpose. Inside, the upright waits with three sticky keys and one song I haven't finished. Outside, the

alley forgets to be a threat.

When she drifts to bed, I clear the cups

and slide the piano's fallboard down.

Something catches. A corner of paper,

jammed above middle C. I ease it free.

Briarbank Pop-Up Studio, the flyer reads.

Below the logo, an address bold as a bruise:

Unit 3, 11 Harrow Street.

There's handwriting across the margin in

the tidy, practiced hand Noor keeps

photographing.

See you soon, angel.

From the hall, the smoke alarm gives one

polite, exploratory chirp. Then another.

Chapter Forty-Four:

Emerald

The piano in the office has survived more spilled beer than a ship. On quiet nights, Chase leaves the lid open like an invitation and I pretend I don't know it's for me.

Tonight, the bar hums low. Emily's taken Charlie and Rosaleigh for hot chips and a movie crop-dusted in popcorn salt. Jesse ghosts the floor, a wall with breath. Eli dry-polishes the same glass like it can forget him back.

Chase taps the bench. "Five minutes," he says. "Call it scales."

It isn't scales. It's a road my fingers learn by headlights. He follows with the left hand, laying down a path I can trust. The notes puddle green in the half-light, emerald in my ears. Ribs loosen. Shoulders forget their job.

"Again," he murmurs. Not a drill. A prayer.

We find each other in the elbow room between chords. Close, not crowding. After the last note, we're breathing the same air and the quiet has its own gravity.

"Cas." Soft, certain. He looks at my mouth the way you look at a coastline you've always wanted to walk and never had the right shoes for.

I should step back. I don't. His hand finds the back of my neck and I don't flinch. The first brush of his mouth is gentler than my fear.

The office door bangs. "Found you," Amelia sings, sugar over steel. Eli slouches in behind her, a bad moon towing worse weather.

Chase straightens. Amelia's eyes flick from my mouth to his, inventory complete. "Cute," she says, too bright. "Since we're trading surprises—" the smile goes surgical "—I'm late."

The word lands like a match.

Chase's jaw ticks like a broken metronome. "We'll talk," he says, steady as a lie you tell a cliff edge.

Eli leans on the jamb, watching me watch them, lips shiny with drink. "Congrats, big man," he drawls to Chase, then looks at me. "Guess you're not as untouchable as the posters say."

The bench squeals when I stand. "Out," I tell them, because if I don't pick a door this second, I'll drown in this room. Amelia's laugh sticks to my skin like cordial. Eli's grin says he thinks we share a secret. We don't.

When the door shuts, Chase opens his mouth. I put a hand up. "Walls," I say. "I need them. For now."

He looks like a man who'll stay on the outside of a burning house if that's where I say the door is. He nods once. "Then I wait."

I take the stairs and the cold and the night like a punishment I didn't earn.

Under the security light, a figure pauses across the street. Cap low. A flash of green when the tram rattles by—a brown shard inside it like lightning trapped. Ghosts have good timing. I touch the old seatbelt arc and count—one… five… one—then go home anyway.

I bag the moment, text Noor a

summary—door, interruption, figure, eyes—

and file myself back into breath.

Detective Noor's POV: Fault Lines

I don't drink the bar coffee. I bring my own in a chipped mug that says *WORLD'S OKAY-EST AUNTIE* and never explain. I show up with files and ask for a room with a door.

"We pulled camera," I tell them, flipping stills onto Emily's desk like cards in a game everyone hates. "Your alley. Your building. The tram stop. Someone's testing your fences."

Grain. A tall man crossing the frame, brim down. Reflection in *Take Flight*'s window—cheekbone suggestion, beard shadow, eyes catching light. A smear of brown glitches across green.

Cas goes wrong in the way people do when history finds a mirror.

"We also found a partial on the first sleeve." I slide the photocopy. "Cold set hit—trespass and vandalism, years back. Cautioned." Backside: a staff card in tidy hand.

ROWAN ELLIS.

"He teaches at Charlie's school," Cas says, like a door just hit her tongue.

"Then we move like surgeons," I say. "Not cowboys."

Later, after forms and the right questions, I stand at the window. The street opens like a patient on a table.

"I know the sound grief makes in a car," I say.

"What?"

"Highway sixteen," I keep my eyes on glass. "Your parents. Six months in uniform. I held a little girl's hand on the shoulder while SES cut the door." A beat. "She wouldn't let go of a blanket with a rabbit on it."

Cas sits like time let go of her knees. I keep my voice even. "Some nights you don't solve. You just hold the living until they remember how to stand." I palm the mug. The auntie joke isn't funny today. "I'll move like a surgeon. You—breathe."

"Charlie," she whispers.

"She counted to me," I say. "Out loud. All the way to a hundred. Said if she got there, you'd wake up." My mouth almost smiles. "You did."

"Why didn't you tell us?"

"You didn't need another ghost," I say. "You needed a cop." I tap the file. "You need one now."

Detective Noor — Case Log:

- Harrow Street connection recurs. Unit 3, 11 Harrow Street = Briarbank pop-up address.

- Partial print: matches cautioned vandalism (Rowan Ellis). Flag: current employment, school access revoked pending.

- CCTV: male, tall, cap, reflective window capture shows heterochromia artifact (green w/ brown streak). Low-confidence ID; maintain.

- Letters ("angel") show practiced hand, consistent "y" loop; ink weight stable.

- Liaise w/ Ms. Patel (documentation strong).

- Patrols increased around bar + residence. Cameras requested.

- Do not let them be alone at doors.

Keys. Locks. Latches.

Charlie's POV: Green Ribbon

(I)

Ms. Patel says art is seeing the same thing as everyone else and drawing the bit nobody noticed. Mr Rowan says draw the obvious so hard it stops being obvious and starts being true. Both can be right. Annoying.

He keeps the room warm. Every other heater at school is "awaiting maintenance," which means "learning to nest spiders." His is a greenhouse. He wears rolled sleeves and ink smudges and remembers when I switch from HB to 2B without looking. He says I have a point of view. People don't usually hand that to you like a gift.

Year Ten girls called me freak. One said my eyes make her feel "watched by a cat." I told her cats are gods in some places. She shoved me. Mr Rowan separated us with a voice that makes people obey.

After, he said I could stay. I wanted to. He put on old music that crackled like bacon and we drew without talking until the room went quiet in the way that fixes you. He said, "People are cruel to what they don't understand." I said, "I'm not a museum exhibit." He said, "No, you're the artist," and I felt seen. Relief is also a trap sometimes.

(II)

Cas said tonight that sometimes bad men look like teachers. She said his name like it burned—Rowan. Detective Noor is checking. Cas asked me to be careful without saying don't go. I said I'm not a child. She said exactly. It felt like trust and also like a weight.

I wanted to rip every drawing. I wanted to sleep under the bed. I wanted to punch the moon.

I went to the art room anyway and told him I can't stay late anymore. He said okay. His mouth didn't fall. He didn't reach. "Bring me whatever you draw at home," he said.

Today the warmth felt like a thermostat's lie. I drew circles, then thorns around circles, then boxes to contain the thorns. He texted *Composition* under the party banner last week. Today he said nothing. His eyes did the talking—too careful. Hands that hover.

I said I might quit. He stared at my hands. "You'll hate yourself in three months if you do." He wasn't wrong. I left without promising.

On the steps I put my sketchbook face-down so the paper could breathe. The part of me that loves drawing wants to throw every pencil away so none of his words live in my lines. The steel part says no—he doesn't get my hands too.

I message Cas: *Studio tonight. With or without you.* Then I add *I'm not prey*, because sometimes you have to say a true thing before it feels true. I sharpen three pencils. I pick the one that smudges less. I draw the obvious so hard it turns true: ribbon, ring rope, a girl the wrong size and exactly right. I sign with the small signature I'm still practicing. I go back in. The room is still warm. So am I.

(III)

Two girls cornered me by the bike racks. One held my bag; one held my hair. They said I think I'm special because a teacher likes me. I said he likes everyone. They laughed like cockatoos—loud, stupid, cruel.

I didn't cry. Jesse appeared like a wall with shoes. He didn't touch anyone. He just stood there, big and breathing, and the girls evaporated.

He walked me to the tram. He didn't say tell Cas; he knew I would. He said, "If anything feels wrong, we bellow. Loud."

That night I drew a rabbit with a ribbon and stapled it to the fridge. Staple crooked. Ribbon green. It still holds.

Chapter Forty-Five

Alley

The panic attack arrives on a clear day because that's how they like to work—polite and murderous. I'm at the bins behind the bar, breaking down cardboard, when a motorbike backfires like a shot.

I'm under the metal stairs before my brain catches up. Breath claws. Vision tunnels. Hands go to my throat like a body remembering the wrong lesson. The present becomes a room with no doors.

"Cas." Eli's voice, close but not too close. He sits on the concrete a metre away and holds up his hands like he's at a zoo and I'm the sign that says *don't feed*. "With me. Count."

"I know how," I rasp. It doesn't matter.

"Do it anyway." Four in. Six out. Again. His voice threads the bad static and makes a path. He doesn't touch me. He doesn't say *you're okay*. He says, "I'm here," until the tunnel puts in windows and the air stops tasting like metal.

After, my hands shake like cheap fluorescents. He slides off his hoodie and sets it beside me like a blanket without permission. "You saved me," he says, guilty-quiet. "I'm practicing."

It's intimacy that isn't sex and isn't story. It lets two people exist next to a bin without pretending they're not broken.

When I can stand, he doesn't grab my arm. He walks in my shadow until the sun eats it. "Text me when you get home," he says, and for once I do.

That night I check the back-door camera Noor's crew installed. A moth smacks the lens and becomes a monster. The bin still wears its

new caution tape like jewellery. I breathe until

the noise in my bones agrees to be tide again.

Chapter Forty-Six:

Want Nothing Together

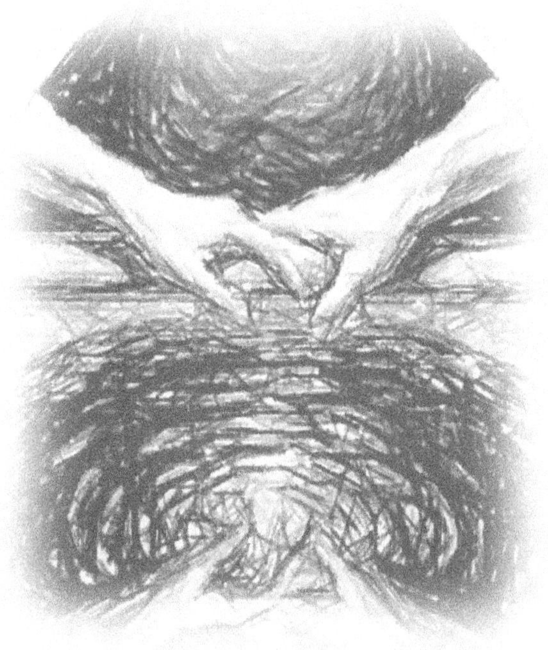

The pit isn't a place so much as a scar the city forgot to stitch—an unfinished excavation where rain collects oil and secrets. At night it's a pupil in the block's face, a dark circle reflecting whatever stares down. People dump things over the fence—trolleys, regrets—and the water keeps its own ledger.

I go there when the noise in my head needs a larger room. After Emily's apology cracked open—sorry for making me carry her and then punishing me for catching it; sorry with a test strip softening the air—after Jesse's face did that men-not-crying thing until it did, I walked. Cleanup could wait. Congratulations could wait. The part of me that wanted to be happy and the part that wanted to lie down in the alley and drink sky could both wait.

Chase was already there, bootheels hooked on the bottom rail, elbows on knees. Sodium light drew an outline.

"You stalking me, Marshall?" I said.

"Left a thing here," he said. "Thought I might find it."

"What thing?"

"My last good decision." A glance. "Nope. Still gone."

I climbed up beside him, shoulders not touching. The pit held the city like a coin—warped, beautiful, a little untrue. Oil rainbowed the surface, pretty if you didn't know.

"They're having a baby," I said. The water edited it for hope.

"Yeah." He exhaled. "Heard the cheer squad in the lane."

"I am happy." I said. "And I am something else."

"Both can be true." He handed me his bottle of nothing—tap water because he's trying to be better at the hours that hate better. I drank. It tasted like bar bathroom and every promise I've made myself.

A siren stitched across the night. We watched it stitch and unspool. The pit didn't care.

"I keep seeing his eyes," I said before I could decide not to. "Bottle-glass green. Brown lightning in the middle."

"Breathe with me." He counted where I could see. In four. Hold four. Out six. By the third round, the city shifted an inch and lined up with itself.

"Look," he tipped his chin at the water. "What do you see?"

"My reflection."

"What else?"

"Oil. A trolley. Three regrets."

He laughed—the first good note of a song you forgot. "What else?"

I stared until dark gave up shapes. A drowned cone. A ghost moon. My face, kinder. "A way out if I jump," I said, too honest.

He didn't say don't. He said, "Or sit with me."

We sat. The fence hummed. A possum tried on a laugh. We didn't fill the silence with how-fine-we-are.

"Tell me who I am to you," he said, not looking.

"You're the first person who didn't ask me to be smaller or easier. A door that doesn't stick. The voice that tells me to breathe when I forget how."

He swallowed, loud as a coin in a cup. "You're the sharpest person I know—compliment and insult. The one I'd call if I'd done something terrible and the one, I'd call if I wanted to do something good. You're…the place."

We let that sit. It left a light mark.

"I told them," I said. "About Sam. The baby. The lie I lived in like a house with the windows painted shut."

"How'd it go?"

"As well as truths do." My fingers found the pale seatbelt arc. "I wanted to be only happy. I can in the morning. Tonight, I wanted…" Too many endings.

"You did the whole job," he said, hitting me up the spine with words he shouldn't know. "You saved who you could. Then told the truth. That's the list."

I didn't know I was crying until I was. Not messy—just a steady leak, landlord roof. He shifted. Our shoulders touched—electric fence. I didn't move. Neither did he.

"Can I—" he started, and didn't ask. His hand covered mine on the cold rail, warm and rough. Our hands shimmered in the oil-black mirror. For a second the reflection looked too close, too real; my body tightened like a fist.

He kept his hand soft. "We can stay here. Or count. Or critique how the jukebox only knows eight songs and loves six too much."

"Count," I said. The stray dog of panic lay down.

"Sometimes I think I'm bad luck," I told the dark.

"Sometimes I think I'm a hammer and everything's a nail," he said. "We're both wrong. And even if we're not, hammers are useful and 'luck' is a story people tell when they don't want to do the math."

"What's the math?"

"You're here," he said. "I'm here." He squeezed once, punctuation. "That's the math that matters."

He finally looked at me, tender and fierce at once. His hand hovered near my cheek like we were gas and he'd learned about sparks. "I'm not asking for anything," he said. "Not tonight. Not ever if you don't want it. I just want you to have somewhere soft to fall when you're tired of being so damn sharp."

"I don't know what I want," I said—lie and truth.

"Okay. We can want nothing together."

We sat in the impossible sentence. A train passed; the water shivered. My phone buzzed with messages I'd read later.

"Tell me something good," I asked, greedy.

"There's this kid who buys the same ice-cream every Friday," he said. "Last week he brought his grandma and said, 'This is the place that knows me.' I want to be that. For someone. For you." He winced. "Less weird in my head."

"Exactly right," I said, surprising us both by leaning in that last inch. My head found the space under his jaw like it had been saved. We stayed there, breathing the same measured air. Not a kiss, not-not a kiss—just the kind of touch that hacks your lungs and rewrites your living instructions.

"If we do this," I said, because I am always a contract, "we do it slow."

"Snail pace. Glacier. Geologic time."

"Don't get cocky."

"Never," he lied.

We counted once more. On the last out my breath snagged—two lights in the pit, green as old glass, too bright for trick water. I tensed, forced the exhale.

"What?" he asked.

"Nothing," I said, refusing to give every ghost a chair. "Let's get back. There's a bar to close."

We jumped down. The fence hummed like it approved.

Two blocks later the first thin lick of smoke found us.

We looked up together.

The night tilted. We ran.

The Almost

A week later they move the upright to the quiet corner because someone decided live music sells more mulled wine, even in Australian summer. The room glows. I glow a little. Chase plays a carol that forgot to be sincere. Our shoulders touch. The whole bar softens into a single chord.

"I haven't stopped thinking about the office," he says.

"Me neither," I admit, because truth is easier when there's music to hold it up.

His knuckles brush mine on the keys. That's all it takes to undo a person. We're a breath from a thing you can't roll back when the back-door glass shivers. In the reflection: Amelia, a hinge of a smile; Eli at her shoulder, weather you can smell.

The chord dies. I put the walls up so hard my ribs complain. Chase's face closes like a book that thought it might get to stay open. We play the next song. We don't sing.

After close, we stand at the curb with our coats pretending Melbourne winter. The city hums the safe songs—trams, late talk, a siren that doesn't mean us. We say goodnight like we mean to survive each other. I turn toward home. He lingers under the awning with the shortbread tin he keeps bringing back like an apology.

Two blocks from Take Flight, a thin lick of smoke finds me. It tastes like something that wants to be a memory. I look back.

Across the street, a light flickers in the office window we left dark. Then another.

The security light hiccups. The alley glows wrong.

I run.

The back door is warm, then hot. The lock sticks like a story that doesn't want the next chapter. I swear, kick the bar—once, twice—and it gives. Smoke breathes out like a kept secret.

"Fire service en-route," someone shouts behind me. Eli? Jesse? My name folds in the heat. Chase is suddenly there—of course he is—shoulder to shoulder without touching. "Stay low," he says, and it isn't a suggestion.

We drop. The office is a mouth full of black. The upright leans in silhouette, lid up, fallboard ajar. A paper curls on the stand, burning from one corner—music I know by shape, not by notes.

Emerald.

Heat skates my face. The flame walks the stave like it knows the way home. Something else tight to the fallboard browns, then blackens—a small rectangle taped there like a plaque.

I crawl closer, sleeve over mouth, lungs already bargaining. The tape lets go; the card flutters to the floor between us, ember-lit.

See you soon, angel.

A second flame blooms to our left. Through the smoke the piano's green ribbon of sound turns to the wrong colour—orange, hungry. The building inhales.

Somewhere under the alarms, my phone vibrates against my thigh. One line ghosts the lock screen before the smoke erases it.

CHARLIE: Pin—Unit 3, 11 Harrow Street—

The roof cracks like a knuckle. The world goes bright.

Chapter Forty-Eight:

Ashes

The first siren sounds like a yawn. The second shrieks. By the third, the city is a throat clearing.

"Take Flight," Jesse says into my phone, voice gone flat. "Alarms tripped."

We're already moving. Keys. Shoes. Charlie at the door, white around the mouth. "Stay with Sam," I tell her. She shoves Rosaleigh's bunny into my hands like a blessing and nods like a soldier.

The strip is a mouth of smoke. Fire eats windows and turns glass to glitter. Blue tape, barking orders, heat like a wall. Jesse pins me back. Emily snaps *No* into my ear like a command for the fire itself.

A hand clamps my shoulder—Detective Noor, calm steel. "Stay behind the tape."

"Chase is inside," I manage. She signals to a firefighter; language I'm not allowed to know.

Her radio cracks another world open: "Unit twelve, welfare check, possible ten-fifty-six—male, mid-thirties. Address… Briarbank, Unit 3 11 Harrow Street." A beat. "Caller identified as Amelia Harris."

Jesse goes still. "Eli," he breathes. Emily's eyes find Noor's. Fast math.

Noor tosses keys to her unmarked and doesn't look away from the fire. "Lights on. Call me from the door. Don't be heroes alone."

They vanish in blue.

Minutes stretch. A groan, a shout that isn't instruction. Firefighters spill into the alley with a blackened weight between them.

Paramedics descend: bag, mask, compressions—language that makes air thin. A blanket shields the face. No one says a name. Ambulance doors slam. It pulls away steady, unmerciful. Alive? Dead? The street refuses to answer.

My phone vibrates against my thigh. Smoke-smeared screen. One line ghosts the lock:

CHARLIE: Pin—Unit 3, 11 Harrow Street—

Static eats the rest. The roof cracks like a knuckle. Glass sighs.

Noor's phone spits Emily's voice in bursts—"we found—he's—breathing—no—wait—" then static. Another siren, far off, braids with ours. Two gurneys, two directions, two men I can't stop loving in two different ways.

"Cas," Noor says, gentler than any siren. "We go to the hospital. We wait."

The tape snaps in the wind. The bar smoulders. Smoke turns the streetlight into a moon. I grip the green ribbon on the rabbit until it cuts crescent moons into my palm.

Movement at the end of the lane. A figure just outside the cordon. Head tipped. Watching. When the light hits, the eyes flash green with a jagged brown streak—lightning caught in glass—or maybe it's just shadow and someone holding up a phone, Amelia's face a pale coin behind it.

Rowan? Amelia?

The night doesn't say.

The city opens its mouth. We step in.

Interlude — Detective Noor: Incident Log

Case: Take Flight Structure Fire / Related Persons of Interest

- Time of alarm: 21:47.

- Point of origin: office (rear). Preliminary: ignition at upright piano, fallboard open, sheet music partially consumed.

- Evidence recovered: scorched note adjacent to fallboard—"See you soon, angel." Bagged. Consistent looped "y," stable ink weight (matches prior letters).

- CCTV pulls: alley cam (smoke distortion); tram stop cam shows tall male, cap, partial face in reflection—possible heterochromia artifact (green w/ brown streak). Confidence low; keep as working hypothesis.

- Parallel call: 21:51, welfare check to Unit 3,

11 Harrow Street, Briarbank, post (caller: Amelia Harris). Male located conscious, intoxication + superficial lacerations; transported.

• Harrow St Unit 3 ping received from Charlie Marshall 21:49 (partial). Geofence request submitted.

• School matter (Rowan Ellis) linked via partial print on first letter (old caution). Employment suspended; pop-up studio observed at Briarbank Arts precinct.

• Actions: patrols extended to residence + bar; canvass Briarbank units; seize Take Flight DVR; interview A. Harris + E. North; request school HR file for R. Ellis; notify Ms. Patel.

• Note to self: Do not let Cas or Charlie approach Harrow/Briarbank addresses without police presence. Doors. Keys. Latches.

Charlie's POV: Waiting Room Maths

Hospitals are made of beige and waiting. Fluorescents hum like they're bored. A TV shows a beach and no one looks at it.

Rosie is asleep on my lap in the world's stupidest position, starfish with a rabbit. I should move her. I won't. Her breath is a metronome. I count because counting is a spell we know.

I make a list the way Ms. Patel taught me to start light and then press darker when I'm sure:

- 1 siren — maybe a drill.
- 2 — not a drill.
- 3 — ours.

I texted Cas the pin—Harrow Street— right before the roof noise. The message shows one tick. I stare at the grey tick like I can make it turn blue with rage. I cannot.

Sam buys a vending-machine sandwich and pretends it's for him. He tears off the crust and puts it in my hand like Dad used to when he thought he was subtle. I eat it so he'll stop doing that face.

Jesse texts me a photo of Emily's shoe on a hospital linoleum because that's his way of saying: we're here, we don't leave. He also texts: Eli grumpy = alive. I breathe the word *alive* like it's a new colour.

Noor walks in with her shoulders doing that calm that calms other people. She sits without sitting too close. "We'll have updates soon," she says. "You're doing everything right."

Nobody says that to girls like us. I almost cry. I do not. I draw on the back of the sandwich wrapper instead—ring ropes, a rabbit, two doors. I write *Emerald* small in the corner because the song won't leave.

A trolley squeaks. Paramedics talk in numbers. A nurse says a name I can't catch.

Somewhere a phone buzzes. A message lights my screen from an unknown number:

Bring your portfolio. Saturday. Unit 3, 11 Harrow St. 10 a.m. — R

I delete it, then undelete it, then screen-shot it for Noor. My hands shake and I hate that they do.

"Cas will be okay," Rosie mumbles into my jeans, not really awake. "We have superheroes."

"Better," I tell her, smoothing her hair.

"We have sisters."

The PA cracks. A code I don't understand. Doors open. People move.

I count to a hundred because that's how you make the next breath arrive. At ninety-four, the surgeon's doors swing.

We look up together.

NEXT IN THE SERIES

BITESIZE: REDEMPTION

CAS

The lilies came before the body.

Someone must've ordered them before the
world remembered how easily it breaks. Their
scent hits first — sweet and wrong. It clings to
my throat.

The ribbon across the casket is green, rain-
dark and fraying at the edge. I trace it with my
eyes, not my hands. I don't touch things I
want to keep.

CHARLIE

The chairs creak like bones. Someone coughs.
Someone prays.

I count the breaths between each sob — one,
two, one — and it steadies me. Cas won't
look at me, and that's how I know she's

breaking.

I press the ribbon between my fingers until the colour bleeds. Green for calm, for safety. Green for all the times we lied and said we were fine.

ROSIE

Everyone whispers like they're afraid to wake me.

The flowers are heavy, like the air before rain.

I want to ask who they're for, but no one answers. They just hold tighter.

I think love sounds like the space before a name.

CAS

They say peace smells like lilies.

They lied.

Bitesize: Redemption — where the living carry the silence the dead leave behind.